NEVER AGAIN

DELANEY DIAMOND

Garden Avenue Press

Never Again by Delaney Diamond

Garden Avenue Press

Atlanta, Georgia

ISBN: 978-1-946302-12-0 (Ebook edition)

ISBN: 978-1-946302-13-7 (Paperback edition)

www.delaneydiamond.com

I

"Come on! I know you have more to give. You can do this!"

Carmen grimaced as Lionel, her trainer, hovered over her at the bench press. His muscular body barely fit in the dark green unitard he wore.

Lying on her back, she gritted her teeth with the tremendous effort needed to slowly push the free weight higher.

"Don't arch that back," Lionel warned, his shaved head lowering to hers.

Cabrón, she cursed in her head, but she flattened her spine, determined to complete the reps in the right manner because she promised herself to do better. That's why she'd hired a trainer. To push her past what she *thought* were her limits. She hated him nonetheless.

"One more. You got this," he said.

Triceps burning and sweat beading on her face, Carmen lowered the barbell. She'd come this far. She couldn't give up now.

"Last one. Come on."

You can do this, Carmen, she told herself.

With a surge of energy and a small cry, she shoved higher.

"Hot damn! That's it! You did it, baby!" Lionel hollered, voice filled with pride.

He lifted the weight from her grasp, and Carmen let her arms fall to the side. She closed her eyes, letting out deep breaths of fatigue but also relief. She'd done it.

Sitting up, she placed her hands on her hips.

Lionel looked at her like a proud papa. "What did I tell you, huh? Didn't I tell you that you were underestimating yourself? You did three reps of ten that time."

Huffing and puffing, she grinned at him. "I did it," she whispered.

"Yeah, you did. Put it here." He held up a hand, and she gave him a high five.

Later, after she'd showered and changed into a pair of shorts and a fitted Fit Body Gyms tank top, Carmen returned to the bench press where Lionel was setting up the weights for his next client.

"How do you feel?" he asked.

"Right now, refreshed. Maybe a little energized."

He nodded. "That's what we want. You might be a little sore tomorrow because we pushed you past your normal limit, but I'm really proud of what you did today."

"Thank you. I'll see you next week?"

"I'll be here."

Carmen left, waving to the woman at the front desk before she stepped outside. Her desire to get into better shape served two purposes. One, it was good for her health. Two, her family owned Fit Body Gyms, and if you were going to sell the idea of getting a beautiful body by working out, you had to look the part. At least, that's what she believed.

"Where to, ma'am?" Franklin, her driver, asked as he swung open the back door of the platinum-white Lincoln Navigator.

She didn't actually need a dedicated driver, but her father had insisted she bring Franklin with her. He looked more like a bodyguard than a driver. At six eight, he was a giant of a man.

His skin was dark brown and his muscular body had the strength of a tank, but Carmen had never seen him in an actual fight. The intimidating scowl that could take over his face tended to scare people—whether his eyes were obscured behind a pair of reflective sunglasses or he looked you dead in the eyes.

"Back to the apartment. I have work to do." Carmen hopped up into the back seat, and within seconds, they pulled away from the curb.

Based out of Toronto, Fit Body Gyms was the leading gym chain in Canada and years ago had expanded into the northern United States. They offered group classes for yoga, Zumba, and other exercises, personal training, a heated pool, state-of-the-art equipment, and courts where members could play sports like basketball and racquetball.

A few years ago, Carmen's father took the company in a new direction and expanded farther south, which turned out to be a boon to their bottom line. Most recently, they moved into the Atlanta market, and Carmen had begged her father to allow her the chance to prove herself by letting her oversee the opening of their two new locations. Surprisingly, he'd agreed.

It was a test—a test to determine whether or not she could take over the company at some point. At twenty-five, she still had a long way to go before her father retired and she took the reins of the family business, but she was determined to prove her capability to him.

And why not? She had nothing else going on in her life. She was dedicated to making sure the company her parents built from nothing was a success, and one day, her younger siblings would join her at the helm.

The SUV slowed to a stop at a red light, and Carmen idly surveyed her surroundings through the window. Up ahead to the left, her gaze rested on someone she hadn't expected to see at all, and the world came to a standstill. She held her breath in disbelief and sat forward, eyes focused on the man standing on the sidewalk holding a yellow beverage can in his hand as he talked to a woman on the street.

If asked to describe the woman, Carmen couldn't recount a single feature because her eyes remained focused on *him*. A black muscle shirt showed off the breadth of his broad shoulders, which were achingly familiar. Was that really Carlos? Same build, same shoulder-length loose-curled hair secured at the back of his head.

He laughed, turning his head a little to the right. Yes, it was him!

The light turned green and the vehicle move forward.

Heart pounding at her ribcage, Carmen gripped the back of the driver's seat. "Franklin, wait. Pull over. Pull over, now!"

"Is something wrong?" He slid into an empty space two car lengths away and met her eyes in the rear-view mirror.

"No. Wait here." She shoved open the door.

"Miss Reeves!"

Carmen ignored him and rushed out of the vehicle, leaving the door wide open and heading back the way they'd come. Carlos had walked away, his back to her, so he didn't see her coming. She hurried, wondering how he'd react when he did see her.

That sobering thought made her slow her stride. She was a mess, with no make-up on and her short hair pulled into a haphazard ponytail. Even worse, what if he didn't want to see her?

She came to a stop about ten feet away, and with fear trembling in her heart, she took a chance. "Carlos." She spoke his name in a way that was part question.

He turned, and immediately, recognition sparked in his eyes. He frowned, black eyebrows snapping lower over dark-brown eyes that appeared black. "Carmen?" He breathed her name in disbelief.

Had his voice deepened? It wasn't fair how smooth and sensual it made every word sound, especially her name. Heat settled between her thighs and reminded her of how they'd been inseparable, how every time he came near she couldn't keep from touching him.

Her hands started to shake, and she took a calming breath and hid them behind her back.

"Yes," she replied, elated he'd immediately recognized her despite her appearance.

Carlos walked slowly forward, looking her up and down. Carlos—here, real, in the flesh. She took time to examine him, as well. His face was different—more mature and with a fine sprinkling of hair along the jawline as if he hadn't shaved in a few days. He looked like a rock star instead of an artist, but that's what he was. An artist with a gift for capturing people and landscapes in vivid colors on canvas using only his two hands as tools, no brushes.

He wore several black and silver rings on his fingers, and his wrists were adorned with leather and beaded bracelets. The black sleeveless shirt showed off his muscular arms and made his olive-toned skin, which he'd inherited from his Chilean father and Peruvian mother—a mestiza woman of Quechua descent—appear even brighter.

"What are you doing here?" Unlike his mother, he didn't have an accent, having grown up in Toronto like Carmen after his parents emigrated from South America when he was only six years old.

"I'm here on business for my father."

Immediately, his demeanor changed. His body tightened at the mention of the man who had never accepted him as a viable candidate for his daughter's affection.

"I...Fit Body Gyms has expanded into the Atlanta market, and I'm responsible for opening two of our new locations."

She briefly glanced away as she spoke, embarrassed that she had taken such an interest in the company, contrary to the conversations she'd held with Carlos in the past. Angry at her father's dismissal of their relationship, she'd been adamant that she would walk away and forge her own way in life. A lot had changed in three years.

"Good for you." His gaze lifted to a point over her shoulder. "I see you still have Franklin in tow."

With a quick glance over her shoulder, she saw that Franklin waited and watched not too far away.

"Always." She smiled faintly. Rubbing her hands together, she looked around the area. "You live nearby?"

Inman Park had been Atlanta's first planned suburb. By blending old Victorian homes with splashy apartments and newly built lofts, renters and homeowners lived side by side and frequented the neighborhood bars and quaint little food spots.

Carlos nodded. "Up the street a bit. I have a studio in my loft..."

As his voice trailed off, she had the distinct impression he didn't want to share any more information with her.

"Anyway, it was good seeing you," he said.

Pain pricked her chest. That's it?

"You too." She couldn't give up. Not yet. "Maybe, if you're free some time, we could get together and catch up before I go back home."

He nodded. "That would be nice. Why don't I take your number, and I'll call you?"

Was he blowing her off?

"Sure."

"You can add it to my contacts."

He handed over his phone, and she wiped a clammy hand on her hip before entering her information. He didn't suggest she take his number, and she was uncomfortable asking since he didn't offer.

"It was good seeing you, Carmen. You look..." His gaze drifted over her again, as if taking a snapshot so he wouldn't forget. "You look amazing, as always," he whispered.

Her chest hurt. There was so much she wanted to say, but

fear kept her from speaking. She wanted to catch up. She wanted to know if he'd been well. How was his mother and his siblings?

Please call.

"Thank you. It was good seeing you, too, Carlos."

"Take care."

She almost told him to make sure that he called, but she had her pride. Plus, she didn't want to push if he didn't want to get back in touch. She would let him decide.

She walked back toward the vehicle, and Franklin followed and opened the door so she could get in. They pulled away into traffic, and Carmen sat very still, hands clasped tightly in her lap.

She should be over him. She shouldn't be shaking, and the crotch of her panties shouldn't be damp simply from the sight of him.

Carmen looked over her shoulder.

Carlos was walking away. Had he looked back? Had he experienced the same magnetic pull toward her that she experienced toward him? The same desperate need to reconnect?

She kept her eyes on him until they turned the corner and then faced the front again. Her gaze collided with Franklin's in the rear-view mirror before he glanced away.

Humiliated, she could do nothing but stare out the side window because Franklin knew what she suspected to be true.

She had looked back, but Carlos had not.

Not once.

2

Carlos entered his loft apartment and tossed his keys in the ceramic bowl by the door. His Siberian white cat, Sofia, glanced his way from her perch on the windowsill and then returned her attention to the traffic outside.

The L-shaped loft consisted of an entirely open floor plan where there was no real separation of rooms. What he referred to as his living space consisted of white-painted walls and a kitchen that flowed into a dining area, which flowed into a bedroom area in the corner. On the shorter L side of the apartment, with exposed brick walls, was a bathroom and sizeable studio filled with paints, easels, and an old gray sofa he sometimes napped on during the day.

Carlos drained the last bit of Yerba mate tea from the can, tossed it in the recycling bin, and then took a cold bottle of beer from the refrigerator. As he removed the cap and then tossed it, his thoughts remained on Carmen. He couldn't believe he'd run into her, all the way in Atlanta.

She hadn't changed much. Her short hair was pulled back but looked about the same length. She still had a curvaceous body, but he definitely saw more muscle definition, especially in her bared arms. Her trusting eyes, set in a round face, made you afraid that she was naive and could never see the truth of your character—they were filled with such...innocence, for lack of a better word.

Funny he should run into her after he'd thought about her constantly the past few days. Perhaps through a sixth sense, he'd known he would see her and had been preparing for her appearance.

They'd met at an art fair where he'd been painting, near her university campus. It took some time to win her over. He'd had to temporarily abandon his booth and ask another artist to keep an eye on his belongings, but she finally agreed to go out with him. During their first date he found out she was wealthy, an heir to the Fit Body Gyms company. By then, he'd already fallen madly in love with her.

Carlos took a mouthful of beer and strolled over to the side of the apartment he used as a studio. He dropped his phone on the table, sat down, and propped up his feet. He stared at the only work he had on display in the apartment at the moment.

The canvases were lined up on the floor against the brick wall. Three in all, each containing some variation of Carmen that he'd completed over the past few years since he left Toronto. All showed off the rich dark color of her brown skin and the beauty of her expressive eyes. Carmen laughing. Carmen sleeping. And the latest, to the right—Carmen looking at him with love in her eyes.

He gulped, his fingers tightening on the cool glass bottle. He wanted to know what she'd been up to, was she seeing anyone, but he no longer had the right to ask or to know. The thought of another man touching her, whispering sweet nothings in her ear, made him physically ill, but he'd successfully—for the most part—kept those thoughts at bay since they split. He swallowed down the nausea and shook his head in self-disgust.

He'd left her behind and couldn't revisit those old feelings now. They were dangerous. They would consume him. *She* would consume him—like she had before. He had put up with a lot of shit to be with her and would do well to remember she was wholly and completely out of his league.

He set down the beer and picked up the phone. Before he could change his mind, he deleted her name and number from his contacts and set the phone back on the table.

His jaw tightened and he closed his eyes, tightening his fists at his sides. He'd loved Carmen, but they couldn't work.

Not then, and definitely not now. Not after what he'd done.

MIND PREOCCUPIED WITH THOUGHTS OF CARLOS, CARMEN entered her best friend, Natalie's, two-bedroom apartment. Cherry-wood cabinets, stainless steel appliances, and modern furniture adorned the interior, all located in a trendy urban community that included shopping, dining, and entertainment within walking distance. The back windows of Natalie's apartment overlooked the highway and the Atlanta skyline. From here, she could hop in her car and arrive to just about anywhere in the city within minutes.

It was the perfect spot for Carmen to stay while visiting, and Natalie had welcomed her into the guest bedroom on the first floor, which had remained virtually unused since she moved in.

She found Natalie watching television in the living room, which overlooked streets currently low on pedestrian traffic.

"Hey," Natalie said, not looking up from the court show that held her attention. She lifted a hand in greeting.

Natalie was a full-figured woman with long Senegalese twists adorned with gold cuffs pulled over one shoulder. As an event coordinator specializing in night-time events, she was usually home during the day and gone at night.

"I saw Carlos today." Carmen dropped into the chair catty-corner to the sofa where Natalie sat.

Her friend swung her head in Carmen's direction. "Excuse me? Are you talking about *the* Carlos Hortado, the love of your life, the man who left Canada and you haven't heard from him since?"

Carmen nodded, gnawing the side of her bottom lip.

Natalie muted the television. Holding one leg under her, she turned her body in Carmen's direction and gave her full attention. "When and where did you see him? I need details."

"I saw him after I left the gym a little while ago. He lives in Atlanta and has a place in Inman Park."

"Are you two going to meet up again?"

Carmen shrugged and tugged at the hem of her shorts. "I doubt it. I gave him my phone number, but I don't think he's going to call." She felt foolish now. What had she been thinking?

"What makes you say that?"

"Just the vibe he gave off. He wasn't... enthusiastic to see me." It was embarrassing to admit, but she could share that information with Natalie, who knew her better than anyone else.

Natalie had visited the States after she graduated from university and liked Atlanta so much, she stayed. They remained best friends through the years, and Natalie knew all about Carmen's break-up with Carlos.

Her friend sent a sympathetic gaze her way. "I'm sorry, girl."

Deflated, Carmen sighed. "In the three years since we split, I didn't imagine that when we met again, it would go this way. I guess I'm just foolish and romantic and thought that he would sweep me into his arms and tell me how much he regretted leaving me behind." She let out a dry laugh and swallowed down the hurt. "But that didn't happen, obviously. I don't think he missed me at all," she finished in a soft, pained voice.

"Don't do that," Natalie said fiercely. "Don't do that thing where you torture yourself about how he feels. What you guys had was beautiful, but it was three years ago, and unless he tells you differently, I believe that he loved you."

"Then why did he leave?"

"Because he needed a new start. Because he couldn't deal

with your father anymore. You want to lay the blame somewhere, look at your daddy."

Carmen shifted uncomfortably in the chair. Natalie was partially correct, but Carlos had to bear some of the responsibility. He didn't listen when she told him she would go with him, and he just...left her.

"I don't want to talk about him because it's going to make me upset. Tell me about this event that you're putting on."

Natalie's face lit up. She lost her job a little over a year ago and now worked as a freelance event planner, organizing lavish parties and events for individuals or families, but lately she'd ventured into corporate planning and had agreed to put together an artistic event for a non-profit. She chose an inexpensive venue from a company that wanted to make better use of its buildings around the city, thus resulting in a convenient marriage between both entities.

The event would take place in an old warehouse and include music, art, and plenty of food. Right now, Natalie considered corporate event planning a side gig, but if it worked out, she intended to target more of her advertising toward businesses, particularly small firms, because she earned two and three times what she earned with individual customers. Which meant her father would no longer have to subsidize her living expenses.

"Tickets have been sold, food has been ordered, and guess what?" Natalie asked.

"What?"

"We sold out! All the tickets are gone!" Natalie squealed, throwing up her hands.

Carmen let out an equally loud squeal of happiness and jumped up from the chair. She gave her friend a big hug. "I'm so happy for you."

"I know, I know. Isn't that crazy?"

Carmen sank onto the sofa. "It's not crazy because I knew you could do it."

Natalie took her hand and squeezed. "Thank you for encouraging me to step out on faith. And I know you'll be just as successful working on these new locations for your father."

Carmen shrugged, pretending she wasn't that concerned, but she was terrified of failure. At one point in time, she had told her father she was not interested in the business. She had fully intended to walk away from her family to be with Carlos. Since then, she'd done a complete one-eighty, and though her father had welcomed her into the corporate offices, he had reservations. Because of her previous lack of interest, he doubted her dedication and desire to stick around and work in the company.

"We'll see what happens. Until then, I know what I'll be doing in two weeks."

Natalie grinned, unable to repress her excitement. "*You* will be attending the first Chocolate Art Affair by Natalie Crimson." She threw up her hands. "Heyyyy," she sang, gyrating in the seat.

Carmen laughed and started dancing on the sofa, too, genuinely excited for her friend. No one was more deserving of success than Natalie, and she gladly went along for the ride.

Later, Carmen went into her room to get some work done and removed her phone from her purse. She checked the screen and saw she had one missed voicemail from her sister and a text from a friend.

Two hours later, and still nothing from Carlos. Had she taken his number, she would have called immediately to set up a time to meet up again. But that was the difference between them that she'd always been loath to acknowledge.

Ever since the beginning, she'd known that she'd loved him way more than he loved her.

3

Carlos handed over his ticket and walked into the packed venue.

Initially, he hadn't planned on attending the Chocolate Art Affair, but the event had received quite a bit of buzz in the art community, and his agent had encouraged him to go. More of these events were popping up to promote art, where attendees were not only fed, but entertained while being exposed to different art mediums. He considered tonight an opportunity to information gather and see if he wanted to participate in similar ones in the future.

A wide range of people milled about—different ages and ethnicities, art lovers and pretenders. Abstract paintings filled the first room, and attendees stared up at large and small canvases in either wonder or confusion. In the center of the room, several tables displayed hand-made jewelry consisting of precious and semi-precious stones. There was plenty of conversation, and the sound of live music came from somewhere deeper in the warehouse.

As Carlos strolled through, a couple of paintings caught his eye, but nothing that tempted him to purchase a piece. He stopped in front of one in particular that gave him an idea for one of his own works. Crossing his arms over his chest, he studied the strokes and design and then moved farther into the warehouse where the real action was.

He took the three steps down to the concrete floor where a plethora of artists—sculptors, painters, crafters—had assembled, and a band playing soft rock performed on a stage. On the other side of the room, directly across from the musicians, a long line snaked from the open bar and tables overflowed with snacks, including two chocolate fountains—one offering white chocolate and the other offering milk chocolate.

Carlos perused the artists' works, stopping for a few minutes to admire a guy painting a landscape on a semi-nude model on a pedestal. Another sold prints, and still another painted portraits on a ten-by-ten canvas. With so much activity and energy in the air, he could be here for several hours, and he'd be energized and inspired for days—possibly weeks—to come.

He strolled over to where a woman displayed ceramic vases of different sizes on a couple of tables. They were attention-grabbing, and he considered getting one as a gift for his mother. For years she placed fresh flowers in their home, bringing a splash of color into often drab surroundings.

"How much is this one?"

About to pick up one of the vases, the question made him freeze. Slowly, Carlos turned toward the sound of Carmen's voice and saw her in front of a table filled with handmade dolls.

She looked like she'd been poured into a pair of skin-hugging denim capris and a beige skintight blouse with short sleeves. Wearing her hair in a topknot exposed her neck, reminding him of kissing that sensitive skin and drawing in a deep breath filled with the scent of roses. Carmen used rosewater as an astringent after she cleansed her face and spritzed it on multiple times during the day.

The vendor must have answered her, but he only heard Carmen's voice. "That's a good deal. In that case, I'll take two," she said.

He stared at the back of her head, trying to decide what to do. Stay or go? He hadn't called since he saw her two weeks ago, but she was right there, giving him another opportunity to connect.

Carlos swallowed hard. Would she even want to talk to him?

Didn't matter. He'd regretted deleting her number and wanted to talk to her.

She handed over some cash, and while she waited for the woman to wrap the dolls, Carlos walked up beside her.

"Hi, Carmen."

She took a startled step back, eyes going wide. "Carlos."

"Surprise." He smiled.

She blinked, seeming uncertain about how to react to him. He understood, because he hadn't been particularly friendly the last time, and he hadn't called like he said he would.

She straightened the cross-body bag on her hip. "Is your work on display here tonight?" she asked.

He shook his head. "No. I'm only here to check out the event."

"Oh, that makes sense then." She murmured the words, and he almost missed them.

"What makes sense?"

"Well...Natalie organized this event. If you were a participant, she would have told me."

"And if you'd known that I was one of the artists, would you have come?"

"I don't want to answer that." She turned her head so he could only see her profile.

"Here you go, ma'am. Thank you for your purchase." The vendor handed over a brown paper-wrapped package, and Carmen hugged it to her chest.

"Thank you." She glanced up at Carlos. "Well, it was good seeing you again. Take care."

He took several seconds to recover from her abrupt departure, but he used long strides to catch up and grabbed her arm below the elbow. "Wait."

Carmen looked at him with something akin to panic in her eyes. For his part, he almost couldn't let her go. Her soft skin brought back so many memories. Reluctantly, he released her arm.

"Don't leave yet. I... accidentally deleted your number."

"Don't lie, Carlos. You didn't want to call me, and you didn't. If my number was deleted from your phone, it's because you erased it."

Same old Carmen, not afraid to call him out on his crap.

"You're right. I deleted your number because I didn't think it would be a good idea for us to stay in touch."

She glanced down at her sandaled feet, hiding the expression in her eyes. "And now?"

His gaze traveled over her face, chest tightening with the burning desire to be closer to her, to talk to her, to simply stay in close proximity. They came from different worlds, but he'd confided in Carmen more than any other living soul—more than his own mother, with whom he was very close. Carmen had peeled back the layers and learned all about his insecurities, dreams, and desires.

At the same time, she exposed him to so much. Private dinners at fancy restaurants he couldn't afford on his own and how to pair wine with his food. In exchange, he exposed her to his mother's culture and Peruvian cuisine. He bragged about his Quechuan heritage and of being a descendant of the Incas. He promised one day to take her to Lima and to the Highlands, where some of his mother's family still lived.

At his family's apartment, she behaved as if every meal they ate was haute cuisine, the best food she'd ever had. Her eyes always sparkled with excitement, so of course his family loved her, and her enthusiasm made his chest stick out.

"I no longer feel like it's a bad idea for us to stay in touch. I feel like... honestly, I regretted deleting your number. Would you be willing to give it to me again?" He prayed that the Carmen he knew, who didn't have a vindictive bone in her body, would give him another chance.

During the brief pause, she studied him, a frown dipped low between her eyes. He could almost see the war taking place inside her head but didn't utter a sound or make a move, worried if he did either, she'd refuse.

Finally, she took a deep breath as she came to a final decision. "Okay."

Carlos almost collapsed with relief.

He entered her number into his contacts again and then immediately called her so she could have his number.

"Will you be here for a little bit longer? I just got here," Carlos said.

"I got here maybe thirty minutes ago. I could stick around for a bit longer."

"I would like that. We could check out the exhibits together."

A small smile came to her face. "And you could educate me on all the things I don't know about art."

He laughed softly, his body relaxing because being with Carmen made him feel as if nothing else mattered, and the weight of the world wasn't so heavy after all. She'd always made him feel that way.

"So you're going to listen to me go on and on?"

"Didn't I always?"

"Yes, you did. You were always very supportive, and I appreciated that."

She glanced down at her feet, as if embarrassed by the compliment. But what he said was true. She had always been supportive and simply encouraging.

Other than his family, she was the one person he could count on to make him feel as if he wasn't wasting his time with his dreams about being an artist. She made him believe that the talent he had acquired without any formal training was worth exploring and pursuing as a career.

"Where do you want to start?"

"How about right there?" She pointed at a woman drawing caricatures using charcoal.

They strolled over to the booth and so began the night visiting with the vendors and buying gifts for themselves and family. They lingered at some tables longer than others, and sometimes Carlos talked shop with the other artists and explained a technique to Carmen when she inquired about a vendor's handiwork. They indulged in the hors d'oeuvres, and when Carlos ran into people he knew on two separate occasions, he introduced them to Carmen by referring to her as a friend—a classification that didn't come close to summing up how much she meant to him.

A couple of hours later, they sauntered out of the warehouse and waited at the side of the road for Franklin to arrive.

"That was nice," Carmen said.

"Yeah. Natalie did a good job."

She nodded, and in the silence, his mind raced with all kinds of thoughts, the main one being that he couldn't let her go without confirmation that she'd see him again.

"Come by my apartment. I want you to see my work." The light from the warehouse backlit them and cast her face in shadow.

"I would like that," Carmen said quietly.

Anticipation built in his chest. "How about seven, Friday night?"

"Seven is fine." A soft smile touched her lips. Those luscious lips he longed to kiss.

"Good." He was too excited about the prospect of spending time with her alone and was a little embarrassed by how much he looked forward to it. "I'll make dinner—*lomo saltado.*"

At the mention of the typical dish from Peru, her eyebrows raised in surprise. "You know how to make that now?"

"Yes, my mother finally parted with her recipe." He smiled, which prompted the corners of her beautiful lips to lift, too. "I'll text you the address."

"Okay."

"You're really coming, right?"

"Yes, I'm coming," Carmen said, the smile still firmly in place.

The Navigator pulled up, but instead of having Franklin get out and open the door, Carlos did the honors.

"Good night," he said, looking down at Carmen.

"Good night."

She stepped up on tiptoe, and he bent his head so she could plant a soft skin on his cheek. The whole side of his face heated with warmth.

He helped her into the back of the vehicle with all her packages. "See you Friday night."

She nodded, and he closed the door.

Carlos stared at the SUV as it rolled out of the parking lot. A second chance with Carmen. Could that really happen? He touched the spot where she'd kissed his cheek.

Maybe.

4

As Franklin pulled to a stop in front of Carlos's building, Carmen double-checked her make-up in her compact. Her lashes looked amazing, and her lipstick was on point. She'd left her hair loose in fluffy curls that framed her face and curled against her neck.

Franklin rounded the front of the SUV and opened the door. She hopped out and looked up at his firmly set features, which were filled with disapproval.

"This is between you and me," she said in a hard voice.

She couldn't see his eyes behind the dark glasses but knew he was looking at her because his head tilted down.

"Your father wouldn't approve of this, Miss Reeves," he said in his heavy baritone, even heavier because he didn't like what she was about to do.

"My father doesn't have to know about my visit with Carlos. Don't say a word, understand?"

He slammed the door shut.

"*Franklin.*" She spoke in a harder tone now.

"I understand, Miss Reeves." A muscle in his jaw ticked.

"Good. And another thing, you can go home. I'll catch a cab when I'm ready to go back to Nat's."

He observed her in silence.

"I know what I'm doing."

"Very well," he said in a clipped voice.

Carmen walked to the door, punched in the code Carlos had given her, and entered the building. Once inside, she waved at Franklin through the closing glass door, who had waited on the sidewalk beside the car to make sure she'd safely entered the building. He nodded and walked around to the driver's side of the car.

She didn't stick around to see him drive away. Instead of taking the elevator, she took the stairs to the second floor and turned the corner. Carlos had given her his apartment number, but with only a small number of apartments in the building, she easily found his.

She didn't know what to expect this evening and walked to the door, running clammy hands down her hips. Nauseous, her insides undulated like waves. Why was she so nervous? Because she wanted him to like what he saw. Because she'd come here with memories of heated kisses and torrid interludes in secret. They had never been able to keep their hands off each other, and after three long years, she wondered if that had changed.

She'd taken great care with her appearance. In addition to a layered trim and style, she wore a strapless romper that tapered to her tight calves and showed off her toned arms. The floral print hugged her hips and ass, and the elastic waistband emphasized the curve in her waist. In addition, she smelled good and her nails were done. She didn't know what the outcome of tonight would be, but she secretly hoped it included wild, uninhibited sex that gave her plenty of memories to take back to Canada and get her through the humdrum nights sure to follow.

Carmen wiggled her fingers nervously and then knocked on the metal door. When Carlos opened it, her heart thudded a more rapid, relentless beat in her chest, as if she hadn't been expecting him.

"I'm here," she said breathlessly, cheeks heating with the way his dark eyes deliberately drifted over her body.

Carlos smiled as if her arrival was the best news he'd heard in a long time. "Come on in."

Carmen shoved her hands into the romper pockets and walked slowly into the apartment, high heels clicking on the slate gray tile. The first thing she saw was a white cat with a burgundy collar strolling across the floor.

"That's Sofia. Ignore her, because she'll ignore you," he said.

The joke eased the tension, and she laughed, letting him lead the way into the middle of what would be considered a living room, but the loft was one gigantic space with no separation of rooms.

"Let me show you around. Over there is the kitchen." Open shelves displayed glass dishes and small kitchen appliances. Stainless steel appliances lined one wall, with a huge window that ran the length of the sink and part of the granite countertop.

Carmen sniffed the air. "Mmm. The food smells delicious."

"Wait till you taste it," Carlos said with a wide grin. He was in an even better mood than the two nights before. "Dining area, living room, and bedroom," he said, pointing out each in turn.

The so-called bedroom contained a king-size bed with white sheets and white pillowcases in a corner of the loft. The wrought-iron headboard was pushed up against the brick wall, and to the right of it was another huge window that looked out onto the building next door.

"You get lots of light in here," she remarked.

He nodded. "It's one of the reasons I rented the place. It's great for when I'm working." Carlos strolled toward the bed and turned right, which took them to a space that was clearly his studio.

A gray couch faced the window in front of a low-sitting table that looked quite heavy. Behind the couch were an easel and a wide, two-door metal closet.

"Is this all your work?" She strolled over to the different sized canvases stacked against the wall.

"Some. I took those out to show you. The rest are in that closet or on display at local galleries."

She faced him. "I'm so proud of you, that you're doing what you love and making a living at it."

He nodded, his eyes trained on her in an assessing way. "It is pretty amazing. I never expected to have this much success, but the Atlanta area is very welcoming and appreciates art and artists." He angled his head toward the kitchen. "We'll have plenty of time to go through my work, but I promised you dinner. The *lomo saltado* is finished, but I thought we'd start with a simple fish ceviche. Care to help me in the kitchen?"

"I'd love to." They'd cooked together in the past, and she liked the idea of doing it again.

While Carmen washed her hands, Carlos removed the ingredients—sea bass, limes, a paste made of *aji amarillo*—a mild yellow pepper, garlic paste he'd probably made himself, red onions, and corn.

Though half Chilean, Carlos had a greater affinity for the Peruvian side of his ethnicity because he was born in Peru and had grown up under his mother's influence after his father passed away. And with Peru being the gastronomic star of South America, it was no wonder he enjoyed cooking.

Carmen had tasted his mother's ceviche before. Azucena always prepared a mixed seafood version, with not only fish but scallops, clams, and octopus. She served it in the traditional Peruvian manner, accompanied by sweet potato, onions, boiled corn, and fried corn kernels. Very filling, it could be eaten as a meal, but tonight they'd have a simpler version as an appetizer.

"Where'd you get the fish?" Carmen asked, as they worked side by side. She halved the limes and thinly sliced the onions while Carlos cut the meaty fish into bite-sized chunks.

"There's a market nearby where I get most of my groceries, and they have great fish and meat and vegetables."

They placed all the ingredients in a bowl and mixed them together, and then Carlos squeezed lime juice over all of it and stirred the contents again. While the fish "cooked," he poured a glass of white wine.

"Thanks for your help," he said, handing her the glass.

"This is a nice reward for my work." Carmen observed him over the rim of the glass as he replaced the stoppered bottle in the refrigerator.

She longed to run her fingers through the loosely curled hair sitting on his shoulders. He wore a thin shirt, his back muscles evident beneath the gray cotton, while the short sleeves allowed her to admire his ropy, veined arms.

"I've put you to work, so now I'm going to have you sit down. I promise you won't have to work anymore tonight," he said with a smile.

"I don't mind," Carmen replied.

"I insist." He placed warm hands on her bare shoulders and steered her toward the table beside the window. Carmen sat down, resisting the urge to shiver at his touch.

Because of the loft's open floor plan, she could keep her eyes on Carlos. He pulled wide-mouthed glasses from one of the open shelves, and as she watched him work, she couldn't help but wonder how many women he'd brought here and done the same for—cooking and making them feel special.

She chided herself for those types of thoughts. Of course he'd been with other women during their time apart. Once the pain of losing him had worn off, she hadn't been celibate, either.

Carmen sipped the dry wine as Carlos gathered plates and silverware. "Do you mostly have showings around town?" she asked.

"Mostly, though I travel occasionally, too. I get invited to galleries or other events fairly often nowadays." He brought over the dishes and set the table, placing a white plate and silverware in front of her.

"Do you like what you're doing?" She studied his expression.

He paused. "Working full-time as an artist is better than I thought it would be. Literally a dream come true." A wry smile, then he went back to work.

Carmen was happy for Carlos, but a little piece of her heart tightened with pain. She'd only ever wanted the best for him, but her father had made their relationship a minefield that had been hard to navigate. Carlos hadn't deserved his contempt. He had deserved to be admired and lauded for his skills. She was glad that he'd at least achieved a fragment of the success he'd wanted.

He dimmed the lights, which made their voices lower as they chatted a bit more, killing time until the ceviche was ready. Once it was, he spooned a serving for each of them into the glasses, sprinkled on chopped cilantro, and set a glass before her.

Then he brought over a Dutch oven with the *lomo saltado*, the delicious aroma filling the air around them though the dish was covered. They ate the ceviche first, and she rolled her eyes at how delicious the dish, made with simple ingredients, tasted.

"Good?" Carlos asked, a smile tugging at the left corner of his mouth.

"You know it is."

He grinned with satisfaction.

"So, tell me about your family. How's your mom?"

"She's well. She has her own business now—a store importing Peruvian products."

"What? How did that happen?"

"She's always wanted to have a store, a business of her own, but money...well, you know the situation. She was a single mother raising five kids, which wasn't easy. She did her best after my father died, but life was still hard. She had this dream to open her own store and used to tell me about it all the time, but I think she always assumed it would be out of reach. I think she doubted she could pull it off but never stopped saving. Unfortunately, something would always happen, and she'd have to use the money she saved. It was more of an emergency fund than a business fund."

"That must have been very frustrating," Carmen said quietly. She'd never had to save for anything. If she wanted a car, a dress, a piece of jewelry, she had the means to buy them.

Carlos nodded and finished chewing a piece of fish. "It was hard to watch, so I can't imagine how difficult it was for her to live through." He frowned, moving some fish around with his fork. "Anyway, she eventually got the money together and started her business. She leased a place and started importing items—ponchos, textiles, scarves, gloves, everything. A year ago, my sister helped her set up a website, and now she also fills online orders. My siblings work with her. In fact, Jesús has saved some money for when he goes off to university."

"Wow. I'm so happy for your mom—for all of you."

Another wry smile. "I'm glad she was able to realize her dream, and because of that, my siblings have work and my brother can afford to attend any university he wishes," he said.

"That should be cause for celebration, but you look disheartened. Aren't you happy for them?"

"Oh absolutely! It's just...it all came at a cost, that's all."

"What cost?" Carmen asked. She'd stopped eating, completely absorbed in learning about his family and what had happened since she and he split.

He gazed into her eyes. "Personal stuff. I'll tell you one day."

She saw sadness in his eyes, and though she wanted to know more, she didn't push. He'd give her the details when he was ready.

5

Carlos spooned chunks of meat, onion, and tomato next to the rice on each of their plates. Though *lomo saltado* was usually served with French fries or potatoes, he knew Carmen preferred the dish without them, so he hadn't prepared any.

He poured red wine in her glass, but she halted him with her hand. "That's enough."

"You don't like the Bordeaux?" He thought it went well with the sirloin he'd used to make the dish.

"It's delicious, but you know I get sleepy when I drink," she reminded him.

"Oh, that's right." He'd forgotten, though he liked the idea of her getting drowsy and spending the night curled up against him like she used to.

"This is so good, though," Carmen said.

They ate in silence for a bit as they enjoyed the meal. After a few minutes, she ran a hand down her thighs and cleared her throat. "So, it sounds like your mother's business is thriving."

He smiled. He could sit in silence for hours, maybe because he'd grown up in cramped spaces that he had shared with four other siblings, and peace and quiet had been a luxury. Meanwhile, she'd grown up in a large home, her bedroom suite almost as big as his family's entire apartment, so she always needed to fill quiet moments because she'd been alone so much.

Carlos nodded. "I've never seen her happier. My brothers and sisters are doing well, too. Jesús graduated from high school this year."

Her eyes widened. "Oh my goodness, little Jesús?" Her tinkling laugh filled the air.

Carlos was the second of five, and Jesús was the youngest. "Little Jesús isn't so little anymore. He's as tall as I am and has been lifting weights. You probably wouldn't recognize him if you saw him. He's big and muscular now."

"So I take it you don't put him in head locks anymore?" Carmen asked, amusement filling her eyes.

"No way," Carlos said with vehemence.

They both had a good laugh, and then he caught her up on the rest of his siblings.

"Sounds like everyone's doing well," Carmen commented.

Carlos studied his plate, knowing it was polite to ask about her family, too, but he didn't want to because of his history with them. With her father, specifically, but he was curious about the twins, her younger siblings.

Suck it up, he told himself. "And how is your family?"

"Do you really want to know?" she asked softly.

"I do. Especially about your brother and sister."

The twins were nine years younger because her parents had taken a break from having children after she was born so they could concentrate on building the Fit Body Gyms business. Once they were satisfied with their progress, they wanted to have two more children and were lucky enough to have two at the same time.

"So... Charlie has a girlfriend now, a really sweet girl he met in the chess club at school. Daniela is showing lots of interest in the arts. She's really into theater and is amazing on the piano, so of course my parents are fostering those talents."

"Of course. And what about you?"

"Nothing special." Carmen shrugged with one shoulder.

"But you're here on business for your father, so 'nothing special' doesn't seem like the right answer. You're certainly more involved in the company than you used to be."

She swallowed, and he tracked the movement along her neck.

She lifted the glass of wine from the table and stared down into it. "If you're going to say something to make me feel bad about working for the business, I don't want to hear it."

Carlos willed her downcast eyes to lift to his. "That wasn't my intention. Actually, I'm happy for you."

Her gaze met his. "Happy for me? Why? What does that even mean, Carlos?"

"It means this is where you should have been, and—"

"And you breaking up with me allowed me to reach for my destiny and my full potential?" Her voice dripped with sarcasm. Even in the dim light, he couldn't miss the flash of annoyance in her dark eyes.

"That's not what I'm saying." He rubbed a thumb along the stem of his glass and studied the ruby-red liquid for a while as he tried to find the right words. "We both know you would not have worked in your father's company if we'd remained together. You're happy, aren't you?"

She nodded. "I am," she said quietly.

Deep down, he had hoped she'd give a different answer. If she'd given a different answer, that could have been the opening for him to admit he'd made a mistake and regretted leaving her in Toronto. Seeing her flourish without him meant he'd done the right thing, but it hurt because it meant she was better off without him in her life, and he'd selfishly hoped that wasn't true. A punch to the gut would have been less painful.

Carlos cut into his meat and suddenly wished he hadn't invited her over for dinner.

"But I could have been happier," Carmen said in a low voice

—so low, he barely heard her and wasn't sure he'd heard what he thought she said.

They stared at each other.

"I could have been happier, too," he admitted.

"So you regret leaving me?" He heard the tremble of hesitancy in her voice. Like him, she asked a question but was afraid to hear the answer.

He had so many regrets. "I've regretted leaving every day for the past three years."

For a split second, her face crumbled, but she fought back the surge of tears. She set down her silverware and took a tremulous breath. "Why did you leave, and why didn't you take me with you?"

"I told you why I left, Carmen. What could I have possibly offered you? Your father was right."

"No, he wasn't," she said in a firm voice.

Looking deeply into her eyes, Carlos was determined to make her understand. "He was. You can't imagine the kind of life you would have lived with me. I did things I'm not proud of to survive. I stole, Carmen. I stole gas for my car, I stole canned goods when I was hungry, I dined and dashed." His cheeks flushed with the shame and guilt of his behavior. "Being poor isn't noble or romantic. It's hard and stressful. You wouldn't have enjoyed that life with me. Even when my father was alive, we didn't have much. I grew up in poverty, and I'm very clear about its limitations. Then I became a struggling artist, with no real future, and you were—*are*—a woman with her whole future ahead of her, including a successful business enterprise. If you didn't want to work again, you wouldn't have to."

She leaned toward him with imploring eyes. "I didn't care about what you had or what you didn't have. As far as I was concerned, there was no difference between us."

"That's idealistic."

"No, it's not."

"Yes, it is. There were six of us living in a two-bedroom

apartment. Do you know how embarrassed I was to have you see my home and learn about our living conditions?"

His upbringing was never far from his mind, and to this day, he still lived life simply, careful with his money, budgeting and saving because he didn't have a steady paycheck and never knew when it could all go away.

"I didn't care about your living conditions," Carmen said in a dull voice.

"But *I* cared."

She pushed away her plate as if she suddenly found the food distasteful. "We're talking in circles. We've had these conversations before. I can't help who my family is, and neither can you. Just admit you didn't want to be with me, because everything else you've said are excuses, and you know it."

"They're not excuses. I couldn't offer you anything, and I needed to work and prove to myself I could succeed doing the work I love."

She glanced away from him to the night outside. A muscle flexed in her jawline. When she looked at him again, there were tears in her eyes. "Did you love me?"

"More than anything else in the world," Carlos answered immediately in a thick voice.

"What's to stop us from being together now? You've proven yourself. You're successful."

"I'm not where I want to be."

"And where do you want to be?"

"In a place where money doesn't matter. A millionaire, maybe?"

"And if that's not in the cards for you?"

He shook his head and swallowed. "I don't know."

An uncomfortable silence settled over the table, and he didn't know what to say to fix the awkwardness.

Carmen stared at the empty space her plate previously occupied. "Thank you for dinner, but it's time I head out. I'm going to call a cab and go back to Nat's." Her chair scraped back on the tile floor, and she stood.

She moved quickly, and Carlos scrambled from his seat and caught her halfway to the door. He pulled her back into his chest, wrapping his arms tightly around her. Closing his eyes, he rested his cheek against hers and inhaled the sweet, rosy scent of her skin.

"Don't go." He would drop to his knees and beg if he needed to.

She hung her head, but the tension slowly eased from her body and she relaxed into him. When he was certain she wouldn't bolt, Carlos turned her around to face him.

"How much longer will you be here in Atlanta?"

"I leave the middle of next week."

Mierda. That wasn't much time.

"Spend some of that time with me."

"Why should I?"

He threaded their fingers together and pulled her against him. "Because I'm asking." He lifted one of her hands and kissed the knuckles. "I want to keep talking to you, and I haven't shown you my work yet. I want you to see them."

"I *would* like to see your paintings," she said cautiously.

"Come on. Let me show you some of my completed projects."

He continued to hold her hand as they walked to the area where he worked. Now that he was touching her, he didn't want to let go. He felt comfortable like that, and clearly so did she.

"Stay right here." He went to the wall, picked up one of the canvases, and turned it around to face her. "This was a commissioned piece."

"It's gorgeous," she whispered.

They continued in the same vein with the others. He showed her a work of art, and then he explained the story behind it. She listened attentively. If she was bored with his explanations, she didn't let on. She asked questions, and more than once they laughed out loud together.

Finally, he opened the closet and pulled out the three paintings he'd kept for last.

Carmen gasped. She looked from the paintings to his face and back again. "That's me," she said.

"You were always on my mind, Carmen."

A sad little smile slipped across her lips. "And you were always on mine."

He guided her over to the living room sofa in front of the TV and showed her a portfolio filled with pictures of his paintings. They sipped wine and chatted about his work and hers. They shared funny stories from the past and caught up on the current events in each other's lives.

Their camaraderie reminded him of how they used to be, before their relationship fell apart. Before he thought it was better to leave her behind.

Before he'd made the biggest mistake of his life.

6

Carmen slowly woke up, and a few seconds passed before she became oriented to her surroundings. The street lights contributed their brilliance through the windows to the interior of the dark loft. Carlos had one arm around her, holding her close to his side.

They'd fallen asleep watching a movie.

He was still asleep, his Adam's apple sticking out as his head rested on the back of the sofa. She studied him—the hard jawline, the large, straight nose, and the sort of casual sexiness he wore in every act, even while he slept.

Speaking of which, how long had they been asleep? She looked around but couldn't find a clock, and her phone lay face down on the coffee table.

Her gaze traveled the length of Carlos's body and stopped at his lap. He may be asleep, but his body wasn't. Not if his tented slacks were any indication. His left hand twitched against her arm, and his body tensed, chest going up and down a little faster. He must be dreaming—maybe about her?

Knowing that she might be the reason for his arousal excited her. Carlos groaned and shifted, and then his eyes flew open. He blinked rapidly several times, as if trying to determine if he really saw her or was dreaming.

"Hi," she said.

"Hi."

"You were dreaming."

He swallowed. "Yeah."

"About me?"

Stillness filled the air as he paused, eyes intently focused on her face. "Yeah."

Carmen eased her hand down his chest to the front of his pants. Carlos took a deep breath, but he didn't stop her. Her hand massaged his hard length through his clothes while his jaw hardened with the tension exerted to remain still.

"What were you thinking about?" Carmen asked.

"I think you know," he answered in a strained voice.

The same thing she was. Seeing him again made her emotional and long to be closer. Maintaining eye contact, she eased from under his arm and lowered to the floor.

"Carmen, you don't have to do that," he said, but didn't sound very convincing.

"I want to." She loved giving head—to him. Damn near salivated at the thought of having that pleasure again—the weight against her tongue, the width of him stretching the corners of her lips tight.

His face twisted into a brief grimace, as if her actions would bring him pain instead of pleasure.

Carefully, she unfastened the button on his pants. As she lowered the zipper, he stopped breathing completely and his fingers curled into fists beside his thighs.

Carmen grasped the base of his shaft, and lowering her head, she maintained eye contact and slowly circled the tip with her tongue before sucking the hard flesh between her lips. He inhaled sharply, his chest rising as she stretched her mouth over his wide width. She took her time and made a game of teasing him and enjoyed watching him squirm as she licked the veined underside with steady strokes and then blew on the tip.

She moved her mouth and the hand at the base of his shaft in time together until Carlos was panting and gripping the sofa's edge. She moaned as she enthusiastically engaged in the act, which only turned him on more. He cursed loudly and grabbed a handful of her hair, and she tightened the suction of her mouth, sucking hard, gripping him with her right hand while the other gently raked the inside of his thighs and fondled his balls.

Carlos started thrusting, his breathing heavy and labored. "Carmen," he groaned, his voice a warning.

But she didn't want to stop. She took pride in making him feel good. In making love to him and showing how much she'd missed him—how much she'd missed sharing such intimacies with him.

She moaned and whimpered around his dick, little sounds that let him know how much she relished the task at hand. She enjoyed it so much her panties were damp and her nipples hard as pebbles.

Carlos's head fell back, and he let out a harsh curse. "I'm coming, Carmen."

He sounded so helpless—helpless in the clutches of her mouth. She pinched the sensitive skin of his testicles, and he swore again and let out a shuddering moan. Face still tilted toward the ceiling, he gripped the back of her head with both hands and forced her mouth lower on his hard flesh.

She gave in without resistance and let him lift deeper into her mouth. Warm cum hit the back of her throat, and he shuddered as she massaged his thighs and pelvis, wringing every last bit of tension from his body until he wilted into the cushions.

Carmen withdrew her mouth and then sat on the table before him, satisfied with her performance, and Carlos clearly was too. When he finally lifted his head and looked at her, the intensity in his dark eyes in the nearly black room sent warm tingles over her skin.

He pulled her onto his lap and kissed her cheeks, a corner of her mouth, and then her lips.

"You have a dangerous mouth," he said in a low voice.

Mighty pleased with herself, Carmen smiled.

"I need to return the favor."

She shivered in anticipation when his lips briefly touched against hers in a soft kiss. Then he kissed her again, harder and more prolonged.

Carlos stood and adjusted his pants. Then he lifted Carmen in his arms, and she wrapped her legs around his waist. He placed her on the bed against the pillows and within seconds had removed her heels and romper, leaving her almost naked before him in a pair of silky black panties.

Carlos kicked off his shoes and lowered to the bed. Without warning, he pushed her legs apart and pressed his face between her thighs. He took a deep breath and groaned, fingers gripping her calves as he held her legs open.

"Carlos," she whispered, arching her back. His face against her crotch, smelling her, was almost obscene.

He sucked on her through her panties, using his teeth and lips in a torturous move that had her lifting off the mattress. He sucked until her panties were wet with his saliva and her own arousal. His actions were unbearably erotic and typical Carlos. He loved to torture her.

Finally, he pulled her panties to the side and took another deep breath, and she heard another low moan escape from him. With his head bent over her, she couldn't see him well for the sweep of hair that covered his features. His curls brushed the inside of her thighs and added another sensation to further torture her heavily aroused body.

"This used to be mine," he whispered.

It still is.

The words trembled on the tip of Carmen's tongue, but she didn't have a chance to speak because he slid the underwear down her legs and tossed it aside. Then his mouth landed on her with a sloppy, wet sound. He devoured her lower lips like a man possessed, swirling his tongue around and within and then licking his lips, as if he'd never tasted anything so delicious.

The fingers of one hand slid onto the back of his head, slipping into the soft curls and keeping him in place against her center. His tongue glided through the slippery wetness coating her sex. Aroused and aching, Carmen spread her legs wider and let him feast, squeezing her own breasts with her other hand and rubbing on her painfully hard nipples.

The unerring swipe of his talented tongue showed no mercy to her stiffened clit. With her breathing fractured and irregular, Carmen pleaded with him not to stop. She was so close to coming.

Finally she did, her fingers going back to his hair and tightening, her body rocked by tremors so profound her back arched, her eyes closed tight, and her mouth fell open on a hoarse cry of pleasure.

But Carlos wasn't done. He crawled up the bed, and his mouth closed over one chocolate-tipped breast.

"Wait," she whispered, barely recognizing the tormented sound to her own voice as her sensitive body struggled to recover.

He ignored her hoarse plea and gorged on her taut flesh, then shifted to the other nipple and sucked and licked with utter abandon. Every movement of his mouth echoed with intensity at the apex of her thighs.

His hands skated down her body, sweeping over her legs and knees, exploring as if every inch was brand new. But it wasn't. He knew all of her.

He took control of her pleasure, and she reacted in kind. She tugged his shirt and undershirt off with urgent desperation to experience the pleasure of her naked skin against his. She scraped her nails down his sides and over his tight ass—a little too harsh. A little too anxious.

"I want you. I need you," Carlos whispered.

"Yes. Yes," Carmen panted.

He sheathed himself in protection and then gripping her bare ass, aligned his hips with hers and pressed home with a low groan. The entire universe stood still while her muscles stretched to fit the depth and circumference of his solid erection. The drive of his hips inflicted immense pleasure, forcing her to wail and gasp and tremble beneath him.

Carlos had control of her body and used a commanding force of thrusts and hard hands to hitch her hips higher and allow him in deeper. Another moan scaled the length of her throat and escaped through her mouth. She grabbed a handful of hair and gripped one of his shoulder blades, pushing her hips higher and harder against his, running down the orgasm just out of reach.

"That's it. Harder, *mi amor.* Come for me."

And she did, splintering into pieces at his simple command. Contracting around him and turning his smooth rhythm into a manic pace. Her whimpers of pleasure sounded in the room, her fingers digging into the hard muscles of his back. Her hoarse cries swept through the cavernous space. Nothing in life had ever felt as good as being claimed by him.

Carlos shuddered and collapsed on top of her, burying his face into her neck. She wrapped her arms around him, rubbed the musculature of his back, his shoulder blades, and wrapped her legs around his waist and just held on.

Overcome by emotion, she said softly in his ear, "I still love you."

His whispered response was immediate. "I still love you, too."

☙ 7 ❧

Carlos squinted into the bright morning light. No surprise he'd slept later than usual after the night he and Carmen had.

The scent of freshly brewing coffee weighed on the air, and he lifted onto his elbows and stared across the open space at Carmen. She wore her short hair in a loose knot on the crown of her head and moved around the kitchen in his bedroom slippers and the sleeveless white undershirt from the night before. The shoes were way too large for her small feet, but made sense on the cool tile floor. The shirt swamped her body and looked more like a dress on her petite frame, and when she turned slightly, the sides of her breasts were on display.

Humming softly as she worked, Carmen poured coffee into two mugs on the counter while Sofia rubbed against the back of her calves in an attempt to get her attention.

Warmth unfolded in his chest. She behaved as if she'd been there many times before and making coffee Saturday morning after a long night of sex was part of their regular routine.

It could have been, a nagging voice whispered.

Carlos brushed aside the thought. No negativity. He preferred to dwell on the here and now.

He fell back against the pillows and stared up at the wood beam ceiling. They didn't have much more time together before she left for Toronto, and he didn't think he'd ever hated anything as much as the thought of her leaving to go home.

"Good morning," Carmen sang as she came toward him, face beaming and a steaming cup in each hand. "I see you're up, and I made coffee."

"How long have you been awake?" Carlos sat up and took one of the mugs. "Thank you."

"Not long. Long enough to make coffee and that's it." She sat cross-legged beside him and took a sip.

They both looked at each other.

"So..." she said.

"So," Carlos said, a smile lifting the corners of his mouth.

Carmen bit her lip. "About last night..."

"I'm glad you came. I'm glad you stayed." Carlos looked into her eyes.

"Good, because I'm glad, too, and I don't care about what happened in the past. I'm just happy we're here together again. I'm right where I want to be. With you."

He didn't deserve her. She was too damn good for him. "Perfect. We see eye to eye."

The smile she sent him, right before she took another sip of coffee, was soft and sweet and radiated joy. *He* was the reason for her good spirits, and if he could, he'd always keep her smiling.

Carmen rested her back against the pillows, stretching out her legs on top of the sheet. "What do you want for breakfast?"

"Most of the time, I have fruit or cereal—something simple. But, there's a place not too far from here where we can eat. Want to try it?"

She nodded. "I'm starving. We should clean up and get dressed then, huh?"

"Yeah, but before we do, we need to talk."

Carlos raked his fingers through his messy hair. Carmen used to always be the one who wanted to have the serious conversations, while he used to always run from them because he wanted to pretend there was nothing wrong. He didn't do that anymore.

"You leave in four days," he announced, as if she didn't know that already.

Immediately glum, Carmen nodded. "I wish we had more time."

He swallowed back the sense of loss that hit him hard. "I want us to make the most of the time you have while you're here. Instead of staying with Natalie, stay the rest of the trip with me."

Her eyes widened. "Are you sure?"

"It's only four more days."

"Oh, so you can tolerate me for four days, but beyond that—"

"No." He cut her off on purpose, because he didn't want her to make a joke about them. This was real and hard. "If I could have you stay forever, I would, but I know that's not realistic. We can't just pick up where we left off, because you have to go back home, and you have responsibilities."

"Yeah." She sounded less than enthusiastic, dropping her gaze to the white sheet. Almost as soon as she did, her gaze quickly lifted to his, eyes sparkling with excitement. "I could come back more often. I could make up a reason—to check on the gyms, to visit Nat—I'll think of something."

"You can't do that."

"Yes, I can. Think about it. I have two perfectly valid reasons for coming back to Atlanta. I can't come back right away, but maybe in another month or so. In the meantime, we could keep in touch."

Carlos pondered her words for a moment, turning them around in his head. Toronto and Atlanta were very far away from each other, but that didn't mean they couldn't make a long-distance relationship work.

"And I could see you whenever I visit my family," he said.

"Yes!" She couldn't hide her excitement and looked like she was about to bounce off the bed.

Carlos lifted a hand. "Wait a minute. What about your father, Carmen?"

"What about him?"

"Do you plan to tell him about us?" Worry tightened his shoulders.

The light in her eyes dimmed. "I...I might have to keep our relationship from my father for a bit. You understand, don't you? Just for a little bit, to avoid the drama, you know?"

"I think that's a good idea."

He didn't want the drama either, because there was no way her father would welcome Carlos back into her life. He didn't want to look into Alfred Reeves's eyes and see the same condescension and derision he'd witnessed during the period they dated. Carlos had never been good enough for the millionaire's daughter, and he was pretty sure nothing had changed.

"So you understand? Really?" Carmen asked softly.

"Yes."

He took her mug and set both cups on the table beside the bed. When he pulled her to him, she came willingly, snuggling in his arms and resting her head on his shoulder.

He kissed her temple. "It's best, for now."

"I agree. But we will tell him, eventually."

"Eventually," Carlos agreed dully and without feeling.

His hand trailed up and down her spine in a slow loop. This time, he would be ready for Alfred Reeves's contempt. He was no longer a twenty-two-year-old aspiring artist. Though he didn't have the Reeves' wealth, he made an honest, comfortable living. And more than anything, Carmen loved him. She still loved him, after all this time.

He'd messed up three years ago—letting his insecurities and her father chase him away. He would not make the same mistake again.

Carmen stifled a yawn. "I'm hungry. Pretty soon my stomach

will start growling." She pulled away and stretched her arms above her head, arching her back.

Carlos's palm smoothed down the line of her spine, his mind shifting to more pleasurable thoughts and making his bottom head lift a little in attention. "I was thinking we could have a quickie before we left for breakfast." He smoothed his hand up to the base of her neck and rubbed his thumb across her smooth skin.

She sent a coquettish look at him from beneath her lashes. "A quickie? No, sir. I need a shower, and then you're going to take me to breakfast."

She slipped from the bed, and Carlos groaned his disappointment.

"You go first. Extra towels are in the closet beside the bathroom door. I'll catch another nap while you're in there, and you can wake me up when you're done."

Carmen moved a few feet away and glanced at him over her shoulder. "Are you sure you want me to go first? You don't want to join me?"

She lifted the back hem of the shirt, revealed her bare bottom, and gyrated her hips. That quick, that fast, the wiggle of her bare tush inflamed his already incendiary lust and turned his erection into the consistency of a lead pipe.

Hot damn! How did he not know she was naked under there? He was slipping.

Carlos flipped the sheet off his naked body and hopped from the bed. With a happy shriek and a throaty laugh that squeezed his heart back to life, Carmen raced toward the bathroom.

But she was no match for his long strides. Before she reached the door, Carlos caught up and lifted her into his arms.

She tossed her head back, giggling and screaming. "Put me down. I demand to be free of your clutches."

He ignored her request and instead showered kisses on her face and neck as he finished the walk to the bathroom.

They were different. Worlds apart, really, but he'd been

attracted to her from the start, a magnetic pull drawing him to her and forcing him—quietly and against his will—to chase until he caught her.

Now she was his again, back in his life for a reason.

She would never be free of him again.

8

"You're what?" Natalie stared in disbelief as Carmen hurriedly tossed clothes into her suitcase.

"I'm going to stay with Carlos until the end of my trip."

"Why?"

"Because I want to."

Natalie fell quiet behind her. Carmen continued stuffing clothes in the suitcase but could imagine the disapproval on her friend's face. She knew her that well.

"Are you sure this is wise?" Natalie asked, accustomed to speaking her mind.

"I know you're concerned about me, but you have nothing to worry about."

Carmen zipped the bag and then scanned the room to make sure she hadn't missed anything. Carlos was picking her up in a few minutes. Franklin could have taken her to his place, but Carlos had insisted he wanted to come get her.

"I don't like this."

"Weren't you the one telling me that he loved me?" Carmen turned to her friend and placed both hands on her hips.

"Yes, I believe he loved you, but he also broke your heart

when he left Toronto. Have you forgotten all of that in your new lovey-dovey phase?"

"Of course I haven't forgotten, but leaving wasn't his fault. Like you said, my father chased him away. Plus, he needed to leave for himself. To become the success that he is right now. Nat, you should see his work. He's even better than before. One day, he's going to be huge."

Natalie also placed both hands on her hips. "Good for him, but that doesn't change the past."

Carmen sighed. "Look, we were both overwhelmed by our feelings, and we both made mistakes back then. The good news is, Carlos still loves me, and my feelings for him haven't changed, either. That's the best part—that we both feel the same and we get to be together after all."

"But you're not really going to be together. You'll be in Canada, and he'll be here."

"We're going to see each other as often as we can. The distance won't keep us from developing a relationship. Think about it, you live here and you're still my friend. Why can't he and I have a long distance relationship, too?"

Natalie pursed her lips. "You know that's different."

"Maybe, but I can't stop now. I can't give up on him or us. Nat, I feel like a new woman. I feel *alive*." She grinned broadly to convey the message to her friend, but Natalie's brow remained wrinkled in concern.

"You're my closest friend, and I want nothing but the best for you. Promise me you'll be careful and take your time."

Carmen shook her head. "Too late for that. I'm all in with both feet, up to my nose and drowning in Carlos."

Natalie rolled her eyes. "Man, you're such a hopeless romantic."

"Sorry I'm not more practical, like you."

"I wish you were. But can I say one more thing?"

"Do you have to?" Carmen asked with a rigid smile.

"Hear me out. It's been three years since the two of you were a couple. You don't really know who Carlos is now, the kind of man he's become. Once you get to know him, you might be disappointed. I suggest that you manage your expectations."

"Fine, I will," Carmen said with a negligent shrug. "Anything else?"

"What are you going to do about your father? And can you trust Franklin?"

Carmen had thought about that and had already sworn her driver to secrecy. "Franklin won't say a word to my father. As for my father, I'll figure out how to deal with him because eventually, I'll have to tell him Carlos and I are back together."

"How do you think he'll react?"

"I'm afraid he won't approve this time, either," she admitted.

"He threatened to cut you off before."

"I know, but he won't do that this time. I'm certain of it."

"What makes you so sure that he won't?"

"Because the person I was three years ago didn't have much interest in the family business. The current me helps expand the company and is learning all she can to eventually take over. If I can be indispensable to Fit Body Gyms, my father is less likely to throw around ultimatums."

"What if he does, though? What will you do?"

"Then I'll walk away like I did the first time." She'd told her father she was leaving with Carlos, but Carlos had sent her back home—embarrassed and broken-hearted.

"You can walk away? Just like that?" Natalie stared at her in disbelief.

"It would definitely be harder this time, but I'd do it, Nat. I'd do anything not to live without him again."

Natalie's eyebrows lifted toward the ceiling, and then she angled her head to the right, studying Carmen's face. "Are you sure this isn't just some good dick that has you acting so crazy?"

Carmen let out a hearty laugh. "No. I mean, the dick is good, but it's not the reason for my behavior. It's love, okay? One day you'll experience it and then you'll understand."

"There's not a man alive who can have me as sprung as you are over Carlos, and if there was, I'd pray for deliverance." Natalie made the sign of the cross.

"You're nuts. Help me take out my bags for when he gets here?"

"Sure."

Natalie took the rolling garment bag while Carmen pulled the matching suitcase and slung the carry-on over her shoulder. Once they reached the living room, the intercom buzzed and her heart leaped into her throat.

"It's him!" Carmen said excitedly.

She pressed the button at the door. "Carlos?"

"It's me."

"Come on up." She buzzed him in.

Minutes later, she opened the door and flung her arms around his neck, as if she hadn't seen him earlier. He smelled as fresh as a spring day, and the ends of his hair were a little damp, as though he'd taken a shower only minutes before.

He squeezed her tight, obviously happy to see her, too. When he finally pulled back, he asked, "Ready to go?"

"All set."

She led him to the bags near the door.

"Hey," Natalie said in an emotionless voice. She stood with a hip against the sofa and gave a less-than-enthusiastic wave.

"Hi, Natalie," Carlos said, picking up the two larger pieces of luggage.

"Do right by my girl," Natalie said.

"Nat!" Carmen glared at her.

Natalie ignored her and stared at Carlos.

"Don't worry, I promise I will."

He turned to Carmen, and even a blind person could see the love in his eyes. Surely Natalie saw it, too.

"She's stuck with me," Carlos said with finality.

"Gosh, you two are sickening. Go and be happy." Natalie waved them through the door.

Before she left, Carmen glanced back at her friend. There was concern in her eyes, but Natalie was smiling, too. Carmen grinned at her and followed Carlos down the hall.

CARMEN'S SOCK-COVERED FEET MOVED SILENTLY ON THE TILE floor as she walked over to the gray sofa with Sofia tucked against her chest. Carlos was hard at work on a painting, his long legs clad in loose-fitting cotton slacks, olive-toned skin bare from the waist up. His body was a work of art itself, lean with the subtle movement of hard muscle beneath the soft skin of his back and shoulders as he manipulated the paint into the image in his mind.

She sat down and watched over the back of the sofa while he worked.

During the past couple of days, she took great pleasure in watching him work, observing him in his element as he alternated between using his bare fingers covered in paint or wearing disposable nitrile gloves. In the current project, the splashes of bright primary colors looked like blunt swipes of paint but amazingly formed a recognizable image of a house at the end of a tree-lined road.

He was truly talented, and she enjoyed watching him work, his brow furrowed in concentration and light pouring through the huge windows at his back. She knew better than to disturb him during these moments, particularly when he brought his face closer to the large canvas to fix a detail and get the image just right.

Finally, Carlos stepped back and stared at his work. "What do you think?" he asked.

Her eyes moved over the piece in appreciation, but she knew his eyes were much more critical. "I love it," she answered truthfully.

Carlos didn't respond. He continued to stare and then

squeezed a little more yellow paint onto the tip of his middle finger and dabbed it on the canvas. He stood back again and finally nodded, tearing off the gloves and tossing them in the nearby trash.

Sofia jumped off Carmen's lap and sauntered away as Carlos joined her on the sofa.

"It'll do for now."

Too much of a perfectionist, he finished but wasn't completely satisfied. As inspiration hit, he very well might get up in the middle of the night and add more color or change a detail that bothered him which no one else would notice.

"You're too critical." Carmen took his hand. She constantly wanted to touch his skin or play in his hair.

Carlos leaned back against the arm of the sofa and pulled her between his legs and onto his chest.

"Maybe I have something to prove."

"Not to me," Carmen said, twirling a lock of his hair around her finger.

"To myself."

"I can understand that. I feel that way sometimes and have the added stress of trying to impress my father."

"He still doesn't think you can handle the business?"

Carmen lifted one shoulder in a shrug, using the same finger to draw circles on Carlos's right pec. "He still sees me as a little girl, someone to protect, and someone who needs guidance."

"How do you see yourself?"

She looked into his eyes. "I do need guidance. There's a lot I don't know about our business, but I'm learning a lot, too. And I'm accomplishing a lot. I opened two locations by myself."

"I'm proud of you."

"I want him to be proud of me, too."

"I'm sure he is."

"He hasn't said so," Carmen said quietly.

"He will."

"You're so sure?"

"Your father's not my favorite person, but he loves you and wants you to be successful."

Carmen touched the tip of his chin. "I want the two of you to get along this time."

"There's a lot of bad blood and...history between us. He's not going to be pleased when he finds out we're back together."

"I know," she said glumly. She didn't want to fight her father about her relationship with Carlos. Not again. "We'll wait to tell him, like we discussed. It's probably best anyway. I still need to prove to him that my decision-making is sound. Maybe once I know for sure that he's happy with my work, we can tell him about us."

"That's probably best," Carlos said.

❧

SOFIA'S MEOWS SEEMED PARTICULARLY MOURNFUL THIS morning. Carlos sat at the table, and she stared up at him with accusatory eyes, as if she knew Carmen was going to leave.

"She has to go home, girl," Carlos said, almost choking on the words.

The time he and Carmen spent together had been incredible. He worked in the studio during the day while she made phone calls and analyzed figures on her laptop. A couple of times they went out for lunch, and twice walked to the market to purchase ingredients, and then came back to his place and cooked dinner together.

Having Carmen stay with him had been a bad idea because watching her leave would be that much more painful.

Sofia let out another plaintive meow and then stalked away. She jumped up on the windowsill and resumed her customary position, keeping watch on the street below. Downstairs, Franklin waited for Carmen to descend.

Anxiety as tight as a ball of rubber bands filled Carlos's stomach, and all he wanted to do was beg her to stay. She emerged from the bathroom and gave him a weak smile. At the sight of her red-rimmed eyes, his right hand curled into a tight fist on the surface of the table.

She cleared her throat. "I'm ready."

Carlos stood and walked over to her. He took both of her hands in his. "We'll FaceTime and talk every day, okay?"

She merely nodded, and he guessed she didn't want to risk talking or she'd start crying.

"Let's get your stuff downstairs."

Carmen whispered goodbye to Sofia, giving the cat's head an affectionate rub before throwing the carry-on over her shoulder. They took the stairs down the one flight to the main level. She dragged reluctantly behind Carlos, like someone on their way to the guillotine.

He handed her bags to Franklin, and though the big man didn't say a word and Carlos couldn't see his eyes behind the sunglasses, he recognized Franklin's disapproval in the noncommittal greeting and the set of his jaw. Once Franklin put away the bags, he climbed in the SUV to give them privacy.

Carlos cupped Carmen's face in his hands. She hadn't bothered with make-up today. Nude lips and bright eyes sucked him in and twisted the knife of longing that would surely remain stuck in the middle of his chest for a very lengthy period.

"I'm so glad we ran into each other again. This is just the beginning, okay?" he said.

"Don't disappear on me." She said the words as a joke, but he didn't miss the underlying worry in her gaze.

"I love you. You messed up letting me back into your life. I'm not going anywhere."

That made her smile, exactly what he was going for.

"Love you," she whispered.

He placed a quick, gentle kiss on her lips, though he wanted to hold her tight and kiss her hard and long. "Bye, *mi amor*."

"Bye, *mi corazón*." With her hand still in his, Carmen climbed into the back of the vehicle.

Carlos stole another quick kiss and forcibly made himself step back and let her go. He shut the door, and Franklin pulled away from the curb. His stomach pitched low as he watched them leave. He waved and she waved from the back.

He missed her already.

9

Carlos swung his legs over the side of the gray sofa and yawned. Sofia lay snoozing on the windowsill and watched him between slits for eyes.

Miraculously, his afternoon nap, expected to be only an hour or so, had lasted several hours. That was good, because his rest had been spotty at best since Carmen left a week ago. Her face plagued his dreams, and the emptiness inside him wouldn't go away. This miserable state was nothing new. After he moved from Toronto, thoughts of her used to mess with his sleep, fueled by regret and guilt and the very real knowledge that he'd lost the love of his life.

With the sun long gone, shadows filled the apartment, broken up by the street lights outside the windows. He trudged wearily into the bathroom, washed his face, and took a leak before going to the kitchen. Restless and not knowing what to do with himself, he stood in front of the refrigerator and stared at the contents.

Water. He'd have a drink of water.

He poured some from a pitcher and drained half the glass. Then he dragged over to the corner to his bed and climbed under the sheets.

He hadn't expected Carmen to be back in his life, but now that she was, he wanted more dinners, more walks to the market, more television watching, and more of her in his bed. More of her breath brushing his arm as she slept and more of her bright smile lighting up the dark corners of his lonely, empty heart.

Carlos grunted and twisted restlessly. He punched the pillow and resettled on his side. "Come on, sleep. Help me out."

But sleep didn't come. Instead, more thoughts of Carmen and the distance between them filled his head, yet he couldn't help but smile as he remembered her in the kitchen, humming and fixing coffee. Her walking around in a pair of shorts and a tank, showing off her toned legs and arms and looking so damn sexy she distracted him from work. Her climbing on top of him in the middle of the night, one hand braced on his chest, the other cupping her own breast as she rode him to ecstasy.

His dick swelled as his loins filled with an uncomfortable heaviness that he'd have to relieve if he wanted to get back to sleep tonight. He thought about Carmen's soft lips and her soft skin and her soft hair and the alluring scent of roses and groaned.

Carlos rolled over and pulled out a bottle of cheap lotion he kept in the drawer of the table by the bed and squirted a good portion into his palm. He stuck a hand down the front of his pants and covered his semi-erect penis, then closed his eyes and tightened his fingers around his hardening flesh.

His imagination took control then, projecting an image of Carmen's head cocked back, her throat arched in a blatant invitation to his tongue. As he envisioned licking her skin, he squeezed and massaged his stiff erection to get closer to relief.

Impatiently, Carlos shoved the waistband of his boxers lower around his hips to get himself better in hand, but he didn't rush. No need to rush. He wasn't a teen hiding in the bathroom, engaging in an act that had to be completed quickly and furtively before anyone burst in and caught him.

Closing his eyes, he moved his hand slowly, savoring the

moment. His quick shallow breaths filled the air. Using his thumb, he rubbed the sensitive tip and imagined Carmen's hand—

The phone vibrated on the nightstand, and his eyes popped open as he was yanked from his fantasy.

Goddammit. He slammed his hand on the device and glared at the screen.

It was Carmen. The anger disappeared.

He accepted her request to FaceTime. "Hey."

"Hi."

Her soft voice made his loins ache even more. Like him, she was in bed, propped up against a multitude of pillows on pastel-striped sheets. She wore a paisley silk head wrap, and he saw the thin straps of a yellow pajama top.

Carlos normalized his breathing. "You okay?"

"I had a long day."

"Tell me about it."

And she did, telling him about work, the phone calls she'd had to make, her nerves when she had to chastise someone but knowing it was a necessary evil of being one of the people in charge.

"Is the work getting easier?"

"Yes and no. Some days are easier than others, but that's part of this whole exercise of immersing myself in the company. I have to learn until all of the decision-making and daily tasks become second nature, so I'm assimilating."

"You look tired, *mi amor*."

"I am, a little. But I didn't want to go to bed without talking to you first."

Carlos smiled. "I'm glad you called, because I was thinking about you."

"You were? What were you thinking?"

"About how glad I am that we reconnected. About how much I miss you."

"I'm glad we reconnected, too." She briefly closed her eyes, and when she opened them again, her languid expression reminded him of how she always looked when she was...horny.

Noting the odd movement of her right arm, he asked, "Are you touching yourself?"

Carmen's brown eyes looked right into his. "Yes."

"Why?" he asked in a hushed whisper, barely able to get the word out.

"I miss you. And you know I love the sound of your voice."

He could barely breathe now, he wanted her so bad. "Carmen, you can't do that." Knowing that she pleasured herself merely because they were talking would slowly drive him insane. "Carmen." He wanted to sound stern, but he sounded weak as hell. Because she made him weak, and he badly wanted to join her in self-stimulation.

"I can't stop."

She moaned, and that was his undoing. His hand returned to his penis, which had softened during their conversation because he'd done the right thing by listening as she talked. But she'd suddenly changed the rules, and he gladly returned to the moments before she called.

"Carlos," she whispered, her voice sounding pained with longing.

Once again, he stiffened under the clasp of his own hand. This time, though, he had the benefit of seeing Carmen live, hearing her voice, and watching her reactions.

"Pull your top down," he said huskily. "I want to see your breasts."

Without a word, she put down the iPad and he heard rustling. Still on her back, she bent one knee and propped the tablet against her thigh. She'd done as he asked, and he had a clear view from her waist to the top of her covered head.

He watched as she rubbed a hand across breasts and played with the dark nipples. They were swollen and erect, and the need to suck one into his mouth pounded through him like the relentless beating of a drum.

Precum leaked from his shaft, and he swirled the liquid around the sensitive tip as sexual tension tightened his stomach muscles and made his balls ache. Watching her was the best kind of torture. He could see but not touch.

He moved restlessly, hips lifting off the bed with a regular rhythm as he rubbed and squeezed, watching the love of his life getting off a thousand miles away. Touching herself. Moaning and biting her bottom lip.

"I'm right there with you, *mi amor*. Do you feel me? Do you feel my hands between your legs?'

"Yes." Her eyes shuttered closed.

"You're so wet, Carmen. You're so wet, I want to taste. Let me slide my tongue over your clit. Let me taste."

"Yes. Please taste." She moaned, and her head flipped from side to side.

"Spread your legs and let me taste."

She took a sharp breath, and when she opened her legs wider, the tablet fell sideways onto the mattress, giving him a lopsided view of her half-naked body.

"Squeeze your breasts," Carlos whispered.

She roughly squeezed her breasts with a hand that he wished belonged to him.

She turned onto her side, her full breasts filling the screen, and he automatically drew the phone closer to his face in an immediate response to get one of the swollen nubs into his mouth. He stopped mere inches from the phone and groaned in annoyance. He was damn near ready to lick the glass.

She made beautifully sensuous noises that filled his ears as she used one hand to massage the soft flesh and the other to stroke between her thighs.

"I want you to come." Carlos swore as he listened to her pant and whimper.

He picked up speed, moving his hand with urgency up and down his hard shaft. "I won't stop until you come. My lips are on your breasts, my hand between your legs. I won't stop stroking or kissing you until you come."

"I'm coming...*Carlos*."

Her climactic cry was stifled in the pillows, and he came, too, with a loud grunt and shudder. He gripped the pillow as cum squirted between his fingers onto the sheet. Groaning, he let out a shuddering breath that immediately released the tension in his muscles, causing him to collapse onto the mattress with a satisfied sigh of frustration. He'd finally released the sexual tension, but he remained frustrated because he would have preferred to come buried inside of Carmen.

If she were here, he could squeeze her in his arms and breathe the scent of her skin as he buried his face into her damp neck.

Damn.

Carlos wiped his hand on the sheet and rolled out of the damp spot. He'd clean up later.

He found his phone buried in the linens near the foot of the bed where he must have flung it in the midst of his orgasmic rush.

"Carmen."

With a little moan, she stretched and reset the iPad so he could see her face. In the frenzied chase toward ecstasy, she'd lost the silk covering from her head and revealed her hair, which fell across her brow and covered one eye.

"Thank you," she said with a sleepy, satisfied smile. She looked like a woman who'd just had some good sex.

He laughed softly. Sweet yet so carnally uninhibited, Carmen was a seductive combination that he could never resist. What man in his right mind could?

"Thank *you*," he said, swiping his thumb where her mouth was, wishing he could actually touch her instead of the hard glass.

She settled onto her side. "I'm coming to see you in two weeks."

"Isn't that too soon? How will you arrange that?"

"I'll figure it out."

"Carmen, I don't want you to have problems with your family because of me."

She was impulsive and tended to act on her feelings. On a good day, he loved that about her. On a bad day, her behavior was problematic because issues could arise if she didn't sort out the repercussions of her actions.

"I won't. It'll be fine. Don't worry."

"I can't help but worry. You were my everything before, and you're my everything again. I don't want to risk losing you."

"You didn't have to lose me the first time, and you definitely won't lose me again. I'm yours for as long as you want me, Carlos."

He really didn't deserve such love and devotion. "What if I want you forever?"

"Then I'm yours. Forever." A beatific smile came to her face. "I better go to sleep. Good night, *mi corazón*."

"Good night, *mi amor*."

10

Carmen pulled into the circular driveway of her parents' house, a mansion inside a gated community that rested on plenty of land in an exclusive neighborhood with excellent schools, such as the private school her brother and sister attended.

She parked her silver Range Rover, a tricked-out vehicle she received for her twenty-fifth birthday, one she'd appreciated at the time but now seemed ostentatious. Keeping in touch with Carlos made her more aware of the excesses in her life, and though he never gave any indication that he judged her, she often wondered what he thought about her lavish lifestyle.

Don't call.

She physically ached to hear his voice, but since her return to Toronto, they'd talked every day—sometimes twice—once in the morning and again at night. She hadn't heard from him today and knew he'd be busy tonight getting ready for an art show. She wished she could be there to support him, but she'd simply have to be patient and wait until tomorrow to hear his voice and find out how the event went.

Carmen entered her parents' house. She'd moved out months after Carlos left Toronto, leaving behind her mother, father, and two younger siblings to finally live on her own. It had been scary at first but a necessity, a move she was glad she'd made for the sake of privacy as well as an opportunity to establish her own independence.

Her siblings were hanging out with friends this weekend, but Carmen knew her parents were at home because she'd called ahead. Since it was dinner time, Graciela was more than likely in the kitchen cooking, a task she took great pride in and a trait she'd passed down to Carmen.

As Carmen neared the kitchen, the sound of furtive whispering made her pause outside the door.

"She's doing very well now, isn't she?" Graciela asked in her accented voice. She'd lived in Toronto for many years, but her Cuban accent remained so thick some people had a hard time understanding her.

"Yes, I'm proud of her," her father replied in an equally low tone.

"Then you have to tell her. She's come a long way. You both have, to get to this point. She wants to make you proud."

Her father grunted.

"Alfred," Graciela said in a disapproving tone. Carmen imagined her mother placing a pacifying hand on his arm before returning to the task at hand.

"And how did that happen? Because that Carlos fellow is out of her life for good. Good riddance."

Graciela tutted. "Be nice."

"There was nothing nice about that kid. He wasn't good enough for Carmen, just like that other loser she dated. Remember that guy, who had her spending money on him like she was some kind of sugar mama? I'm glad she finally came to her senses—on both counts—and look at her now. You're right, she's doing a great job at the office. The staff respects her, and she's shown me and management that she can take her time and make sound decisions—not be impulsive."

"Why do you keep saying she's impulsive?"

"Because she is."

"What you call impulsive, I call passionate, *papi*."

"Passionate, sure. She let that guy get in her head. She planned to leave us—leave her legacy behind. If that's not impulsive, I don't know what is."

"Why are you like this?"

"Like what? You know I'm right."

"She was young and in love. You remember what that was like?"

"Remember? Of course. Now I'm an old man in love." Her father muttered words Carmen couldn't understand, but her mother did because she gasped his name and then gave a low chuckle.

That was the perfect time to enter the room. When she did, Carmen found her parents smooching—her mother standing before the cutting board with a knife in her hand, and her father standing beside her with a hand resting on her ass.

"Hey, tone it down, you guys," Carmen joked, though the sight of them being affectionate filled her with sadness.

She'd always seen their open affection for each other growing up and viewed them as the ideal couple—an ideal she wanted for herself. She wanted a spouse who would love her hard and sacrifice the way her parents had sacrificed for each other. They were the standard.

Graciela put down the knife. "*Hola, mija*! It's so good to see you." She pulled Carmen into a hug and when she let go, looked her up and down.

Carmen might as well be looking in a mirror. People often teasingly called them twins. In addition to having the same deep brown complexion, Carmen had inherited her mother's petite frame, full nose, and generous lips. Graciela currently wore her kinky hair straight, parted in the middle, and secured from her face.

"Have you lost weight?"

Carmen pursed her lips. "No, Mommy, I haven't. How was your trip?"

"You might have. You've been exercising a lot lately." Alfred popped an olive into his mouth.

"You don't need to exercise," Graciela said, frowning.

"I'm not doing it to lose weight. I only want to tone a little bit. See my muscles?" Carmen flexed her biceps, and her mother raised her eyebrows.

"Very nice."

"Thank you. So, how was your trip?"

When she had returned from Atlanta, her mother was still in Cuba visiting family and had only come back the day before.

"Tata wishes you had come with me and wants to know when you're going to make her a great-grandmother."

"When she's married," her father interjected.

Graciela muttered under her breath, shaking her head, and Carmen smiled.

At six two, Alfred's presence dominated the room with a fit body that hadn't softened much over the decades since he'd played professional baseball. He played in the majors for a couple of years but was cut from the Atlanta Braves and never picked up again.

He moved back to Canada to take care of his ailing father, who passed away after a few years and left him with a small inheritance. With the earnings he'd saved from his days in professional baseball, Alfred took a gamble on himself and opened the first Fit Body Gyms location.

With sustained growth, the company expanded to the place it occupied today as the most successful fitness club in Canada.

"How is Tata? Did she get over that cold?" Carmen asked.

"Yes, much better now. You have to go see her soon. She misses you."

"I will."

"She won't be able to do much traveling anytime soon—not

with her handling more of the business." Alfred spoke with pride in his voice, blatantly mirrored on his face.

Her father had always wanted her to hold a position in the company, and now he was getting his wish. At the same time, Carmen had doubts again about remaining—because of Carlos.

The few days she spent with him had been her happiest in a long time, and she was ready to duplicate that experience, especially after their hot FaceTime session two days ago. Time to plant the seed.

"Actually, I think it would be a good idea for me to visit Atlanta again in the next couple of weeks—to make sure the new locations are running smoothly since the opening."

Her father waved off the idea and went to the refrigerator. "That's nothing for you to worry about. We can check in with the general managers from here."

"I want to. I feel like those stores are my responsibility, and I take that very seriously." When had she become the kind of person who lied so authentically? The untruth sounded so convincing, she almost believed it herself.

"I don't think it's necessary, but if you want to..." Her father watched her over the open door of the refrigerator.

"I do. Going back to check up on the stores would make me feel better."

"I think it's a good idea. Don't you think it's a good idea, *papi*?" Her mother turned briefly from the stove and smiled reassuringly at Carmen.

She always supported anything her children did and knew how anxious Carmen had been, wanting to make sure that she did a good job for the openings.

Alfred smiled easily. "It's a great idea. You should definitely go back and put your mind at ease. I'm glad you're so concerned about the welfare of the company—the business you and your brother and sister will inherit."

Pride filled his voice, and guilt swiped her conscience.

"I haven't told you, but I'm very proud of the work you've been doing in operations," Alfred continued.

"Thank you, Daddy."

"By the way, do you have an escort for the upcoming ball? The time will be here before you know it."

"I've been too busy to date, so I'll go alone."

Fit Body Gyms co-sponsored a ball that benefited sports for underprivileged children—from volleyball to baseball—the event shined a spotlight on the importance of team sports in childhood development. Since the creation of the event five years ago, Fit Body Gyms and other sponsors had raised millions that they donated to sports teams around the country to aid in travel, buying uniforms, or whatever the kids needed.

This was the first year she'd be attending, and as a member of the management team to boot. In the past, she'd refused to go as an act of rebellion against her father, but in her new role in operations, she embraced this as one of her duties. Besides, it was for a good cause.

Alfred frowned. "That's too bad. You know—"

"Well, I'm going to clean up a bit and then come back to help you, Mommy."

Graciela sent a sharp look at her husband, and Alfred shrugged, as if he couldn't help himself. Someway, somehow, he always had to interfere in her love life.

"Thank you, honey," Graciela said.

Carmen hurried from the kitchen. She hated lying to her parents, but it was a little white lie. She would definitely check on the business in Atlanta, and while there, she'd kill two birds with one stone and spend time with Carlos, too.

11

Carmen stood on tiptoe in her tennis shoes, searching for Carlos's car among the many that dropped off and picked up passengers at the airport sidewalk.

He had said he was less than two minutes away, but she still didn't see him. Almost a month had passed since she'd touched him, and she was anxious and impatient to do so again. She was about to call him one more time but saw him walking toward her with his easy-going stride.

His curly hair was pulled back in a ponytail, and he wore a tie-dye vintage T-shirt, jeans, and the same group of bracelets and rings she saw the last time she was in Georgia.

Carmen immediately released her luggage and ran toward him. His eyes brightened into a smile as she jumped into his open arms. Laughing, he spun twice in a circle before setting her on her feet and then gave her a thorough kiss that made her body wilt against him and her toes curl into the soles of her shoes.

"Mmm," she said when their lips parted.

"Finally," Carlos murmured, looking down at her with slitted eyes.

"It's been *forever*." Carmen laced her arms around his neck, certain the love filling her heart must be evident in her eyes.

He looked over her shoulder at the luggage. "You abandoned your bag."

"I don't care. Everything in it is replaceable."

He laughed and rubbed a hand up and down her back. "Come on, let's get out of here before they tow me. I couldn't get close to the curb, but I'm right over there."

Reluctantly, Carmen released him, and Carlos took the handle of the suitcase and led the way to a red, older model Jeep Wrangler with a soft top.

"It looks brand new," Carmen remarked, standing back to get a good look. The last time she saw the vehicle, it had been clean but looked much more used.

Carlos placed her bag in the back and shut the door. "New paint job."

"When?"

He held open the passenger door. "Last week. Get in."

He'd obviously had the interior done as well. The seats and rugs were spotless and had that newly washed smell.

Carmen climbed in. "You didn't have to do any of this."

"I wanted to. I hated that you got into my car the last time, in the condition that it was in. That wasn't good enough. You deserve nothing but the best." He braced a hand on the seat and kissed her, the firm pressure of his mouth warming her insides. "I'm so glad you're here," he whispered.

"Me, too," she whispered back, letting her fingers trail down his jaw.

❧

THE OUTDOOR FARMER'S MARKET WAS CROWDED ON SATURDAY, with patrons browsing stalls or patiently waiting in line to collect produce from a favorite vendor. Carmen and Carlos walked side by side, their arms brushing against each other every now and again.

They'd decide on a meatless Saturday menu, so the basket in Carlos's right hand contained a bundle of kale and a large zucchini they'd add to the quinoa and mushrooms he already had at home.

Carmen sniffed a bar of homemade soap infused with rosehip and coconut oil. "Mmm, this smells good." She lifted the bar to Carlos's nose, and he took a deep breath.

"It does smell good. Not as good as you, though."

He pressed a kiss to her neck, and she giggled, swerving away from his roaming hand.

"Cut it out." She set the soap back on the stack.

He came up behind her and slipped a hand beneath her shirt, spreading his long fingers over her belly. "I think I made a mistake suggesting we stop here. I should have taken you home first." His low, seductive voice in her ear made tiny shivers trickle down her neck.

"You need to behave. People are looking at us."

"Are they?" Unperturbed, he kept his gaze on her and bit his bottom lip.

He looked so scrumptious when he did that, and she wanted to replace his teeth with hers. Later, she would, and she'd get a good suck on his lower lip while she was at it.

"We're here to get food because *you* didn't plan ahead for my visit." Carmen twirled out of the curve of his arm and strolled over to a large table overflowing with corn on one side and green beans on the other.

"I'm sorry. I was excited about your visit, but I also needed to get ready for the festival."

In a couple of weeks, a big art festival arrived in Tennessee, one that he'd attended last year and from which he'd gotten sales and good exposure.

"There's no need to apologize. How's everything going?"

They'd talked at length about his preparation for the event, so she knew how important it was to him.

"So far so good. My agent had some good news the other day. She got me in front on the main stage."

Carmen's mouth fell open. He'd hoped for the opportunity but wasn't sure it would happen. "So you're right there where everybody can see you?"

"They can't miss me."

"Oh my goodness, I'm so happy for you!" Carmen flung her arms around his neck and dragged him down for a lip-smacking kiss.

"Now everybody's really looking at us," he said.

"I don't care. Congratulations, *mi corazón*."

"*Gracias, mi amor*."

"We have to celebrate. How about we stop at the wine store and get champagne? We should probably also get some chocolate-covered strawberries for dessert?"

"How did you manage to read my mind?" Carlos asked.

"Great minds think alike." Carmen perused the table. "How about some green beans?"

"Sounds good to me. Maybe some garlic, too?"

"Perfect." As he moved over to a small tub of garlic, she couldn't take her eyes off him. She was so lucky to have him back in her life.

She started examining the green beans.

"Carmen, is that you?"

Carmen swung in the direction of the vaguely familiar voice and looked into the face of one of her father's friends and former business associates. She almost didn't recognize him. The older man was dressed down in jeans and a T-shirt, when in the past she'd only seen him in suits when he met with her father.

"Mr. Jones, how are you?"

"Great. Look at you. You're all grown up. I wasn't sure if that was you or not."

"It's me."

"What are you doing in Atlanta?"

Carmen opened her mouth to speak and almost blurted out the truth. At the last minute, she caught herself and answered instead, "I'm here on business for my father, following up on the opening of two new gyms in the Atlanta area."

Mr. Jones's bushy gray eyebrows lifted in surprise. "I shouldn't be surprised Fit Body Gyms has expanded this far south. Alfred had an aggressive plan to grab market share in the States. Good for him, and good for you, I take it? What's your role in the company?"

"I'm officially the vice president of operations, but I'm learning the ropes in other departments—purchasing, marketing, etc. I'm learning all I can from my father and the other executives."

"Learning on the job is the best way. Nothing beats it, and I'm sure you're doing well."

"Thank you." She smiled easily, though her insides churned in distress. Mr. Jones hadn't said a word, so she didn't think Carlos was standing behind her. But she couldn't be sure. If Mr. Jones said anything to her father about seeing her with someone fitting Carlos's description, she'd have a serious problem.

"Tell your parents I said hello, and the next time I'm up north, I expect Alfred to buy me that drink he promised. Tell him that. He'll know what I'm talking about." Mr. Jones chuckled.

"I will."

"Take care." He walked away toward the exit.

Carmen breathed a sigh of relief and momentarily closed her eyes. He clearly hadn't realized that she and Carlos were together because he hadn't asked for an introduction, but now she had to face Carlos.

She turned slowly and froze in surprise when he wasn't there. With a quick sweep of the area, she saw him down another aisle that contained small baskets filled with heirloom tomatoes.

She walked over, but when she stopped beside him, he didn't

look at her. He kept his eyes trained on the heirlooms. He picked one up, inspected it, and then put it back in the container.

"That was a friend of my father's."

"So I heard." He looked at her then, his eyes probing, questioning.

"I was going to introduce you, I just—"

"Before or after you told him that you were here on business?"

So he'd heard that much.

"That's partially true."

He let out a dry laugh. "Don't lie to me. You weren't going to introduce us."

"He knows my father. I couldn't risk—"

"I know you can't risk him finding out, so that's why I walked away, as if we didn't know each other." His attention returned to the tomatoes.

Carmen stepped in close and stared up into his face, willing him to look at her and ease the guilt that burned her chest. She touched his forearm, but when he tensed, she dropped her hand.

"I didn't know how to handle seeing him. I panicked."

Her words brought a bitter smile to his lips as he glanced sideways at her. "Don't worry. We've been here before, remember? How long did we date before you told your father about us? Three months? Four?"

She dropped her gaze. She'd known her father wouldn't approve, so she'd kept their relationship a secret. He had never approved of anyone he thought didn't match her financial status. She wasn't proud of her decision, but she hadn't wanted her father's negativity to sully what she saw as something beautiful and special, which she'd wanted to protect and savor.

Carlos caught her chin and forced her to look at him. Blazing anger had replaced the playful light from before. "I get it, Carmen, but it doesn't make it any easier."

He stalked away, and she followed behind much more slowly.

They didn't get the chocolate-covered strawberries or stop at the wine store to purchase the celebratory champagne. They completed the ride back to Inman Park primarily in silence, and when they entered the loft—also in silence—Carlos began prepping for dinner. He removed the vegetables from the tote bag and set them on the counter. Then he banged a pot onto the stove with such force, Carmen jumped.

"Can we talk about this?" she asked, as he moved around the kitchen.

"There's nothing to talk about."

"Obviously there is. You slammed the pot, and I don't like the way you're holding that knife."

Carlos slammed the knife onto the cutting board and gripped the edge of the counter. Body taut as tension wire, he stared out the window.

"I love you." He said the words almost as if he were reminding himself.

"But?" Carmen prompted softly.

His gaze slid to her, and there was still anger there, but not like before. "But nothing. I love you. That's it. Nothing will change that."

"I love you, too."

His jaw hardened.

"I do," she insisted, wanting—needing to erase all doubt. She reached for him, gliding a hand up the side of his neck and over his hair. "Let me show you."

His nostrils flared as he placed a firm hand at the back of her neck and drew her hard against him. Backing her against the stainless steel refrigerator door, he seized her mouth. His free hand covered and squeezed her breast, sending shards of pleasure shooting across her skin.

With a soft moan, she tipped her head back and arched her spine, her whole body contracting with the enormity of her desire for him.

He used his other hand to tug down her shirt and fastened his mouth onto her painfully hard nipple.

Carmen retaliated by reaching between them and stroking his hard length through his jeans.

They should talk about the incident in the market instead of using sex as a band-aid. They should perhaps establish a game plan in case she ran into someone else she knew while they were out together again.

But Carmen could barely think with Carlos's tongue laving her nipple and his hands gripping both sides of her ass.

He lifted her from the floor and took her to the bed. He pulled his shirt over his head and tossed it to the floor and then roughly removed her pants. He kissed her ear and kissed a path down the side of her neck to her collarbone.

"I'm going to spread your legs," he whispered in a husky voice, "and eat you out until you're crying and begging me to stop."

Then he proceeded to remove her panties and do exactly as he promised.

12

"Carmen, it's time."

She rolled away to the edge of the bed and faced the window. "No." Her voice sounded thick and filled with desolation.

Carlos dreaded this part as much as she did. The leaving, saying goodbye, not knowing when they'd see each other again. He placed a hand on her arm, and she curled into a tight ball.

"You can't be late for your flight." He kept his voice neutral even though letting her leave would surely gut him and he wouldn't be able to recover for days.

When she'd left last month, he'd lain on the gray sofa, staring at an empty canvas propped against the wall, numb with misery. Talking to her on the phone helped, but barely. Video-calling helped, but barely. What they managed to do quite successfully was highlight the fact that they were apart, and though he could hear and see her, she was as distant as a dream.

He couldn't hold her in his arms or wake up to her body curled against his. Her tearful goodbyes had only made him feel worse. He'd stayed in that semi-depressed state for almost a week, unable to work and barely able to eat, before he finally shook out of the slump.

Carlos pushed hair away from her cheek and kissed her scented skin. "I don't want you to go either, but you have to. If you overstay without a good reason, your father might get suspicious."

She'd picked the latest flight she could, one that would have her landing in Toronto at 12:29 a.m.

"You have business to take care of with your father when you return. He expects you to be responsible. If you miss the flight, he might not let you come back anytime soon."

"Maybe I should stay?"

He heard the hopeful lilt in her voice but couldn't allow her to do that, though he desperately wanted her to stay, too.

"You can't do that," he said gently.

He tugged on her shoulder, and she fell onto her back but refused to look at him. She stared up at the ceiling.

"I'm working on a few festivals, but I'll come see you in a few months."

Carmen looked at him then, and he could barely handle the depth of anguish in her brown eyes.

She sighed, as if giving up an internal fight. "What choice do we have right now?"

She sat up and the sheet fell away, exposing her semi-nude body. Like him, she wore only underwear. While he wore boxer briefs, she wore a pale pink cheeky with a lace waistband. He curled an arm around her waist, pulled her to him, and rested his forehead on her shoulder.

They sat in silence for a while before she suddenly gasped and he lifted his head.

"What if I tell my parents I've met someone here? I don't have to say who." Her eyes brightened with the excitement.

"I don't want you to do that."

"Why not? I could make up a name, and that way I could come see you without any worry. I'm twenty-five now. My father isn't as concerned about my dating life, not like he was three years ago."

"Do you really think your father will be unconcerned about you dating someone in another country and he hasn't met him? Do you really think he would be fine with not knowing anything about your mystery man?" His words came out sharper than they should have, and her eyes widened in surprise. But part of him was miffed that once again he had to be a secret, and once again she was naive enough to be an idealist about the situation. "I don't want you to lie."

He rolled off the bed. Cold tile under his bare feet shocked his heated system. Turning away from her, he ran both sets of fingers through his hair in exasperation.

"I'm lying now," Carmen said.

"Then don't. Don't lie anymore."

"Are you saying you don't want me to come back?" Carmen asked in a stricken voice.

Carlos faced her. "No, I just...I don't know!" he said, throwing up his hands. "I don't know what I fucking want, Carmen. I just know that this is ridiculous, and I know that you don't seem to see anything wrong with simply turning me into a lie to protect yourself."

"That is so unfair."

"Is it? Because this feels very familiar. We dated for months in secret before I met your family, even though you met mine," he reminded her.

"You know why. Because of my father. Look at how unreasonable he became after he found out about us. He didn't approve, and up until meeting you, I'd always done what my parents wanted. I never lied to them. I was a good girl, for lack of a better word. Then I started lying, keeping secrets, and staying out late because I couldn't stand to leave you. Surely, you can understand why I didn't initially tell them—especially my father—the truth."

He did, but he didn't. Carlos turned away from her and stared out into the night at the side of the building next door.

"And what about Tyler?" he asked bitterly.

A beat of silence. Tyler had been a bone of contention between them, and much to his own surprise, Carlos was still bitter about it.

"Tyler meant nothing to me. You know that. That was my father interfering, and I went along with his matchmaking to keep the peace, that's *all*. We went on one date, and we never kissed. We've been through this."

Tyler, a young man from a wealthy family, had been her father's choice. After Alfred found out about her dating Carlos, he arranged with Tyler's parents for Carmen and Tyler to meet. To her credit, Carmen told Carlos right away, and though having her meet with another man made him ill, he'd accepted it as a necessary evil—until he learned about the follow-up after the meeting.

"He came to your house for dinner. Something *I* was never allowed to do."

Tyler was the right kind of man. Carlos was the wrong kind. Tyler had a future and could take care of her. Carlos had a dream and couldn't take care of himself.

"I don't know what you want me to say. I thought we were past Tyler. Obviously you're still angry."

"Because you didn't tell me everything."

"I didn't want to hurt you!"

"It hurt anyway when I found out," he grated, glaring at the wall next door.

She'd tripped up and mentioned that Tyler had joined them for dinner on a night she hadn't been able to go out with him. Knowing that she'd foregone spending time with him to sit at the table with another man—the one accepted by her family—had been a crushing blow that took a while to recover from.

"I was willing to walk away from everything for you. Did you forget that part?" Carmen asked in a low, emotional voice.

Carlos turned his head to look at her. "I couldn't let you do that."

"Then that's your fault, isn't it?"

Yes, it was his fault. He hadn't been strong enough to hold on to her. His weakness and insecurity had forced them apart.

"Go home to your family. I can't provide for you the way they can."

"I don't care about the money. I love you. I only want you." Tears shimmered in her eyes.

"You're being impulsive and emotional."

"You sound like my father. I'm not being impulsive or emotional," she said angrily. "Carlos..." Her pleading eyes conveyed how much she wanted to be with him.

"Go home, Carmen. I'm leaving tomorrow, and you're not coming with me."

"You're right. I should get up. I can't be late." She rose from the bed, and as she passed on her way to the bathroom, he grabbed her arm.

She looked up at him with doleful eyes, and his heart twisted painfully. She was his everything, and life without her had been hard and lonely. He never realized how lonely until she came back. He'd been closed off, determined not to feel again, and here she was—making him feel all sorts of intense, fierce emotions that took up too much space in his head and heart.

"I love you. That hasn't changed in all this time," he said.

"I love you, too." She shrugged with sadness-filled eyes, all the fight drained out of her. "But maybe it's not enough. The distance, my career at the company, our differences—maybe we're fooling ourselves into believing we could make our relationship work this time. How can we, when there are more obstacles in the way?"

This wasn't what he wanted. *She* was what he wanted. How many times had he told her that she was his sun, moon, and stars? His universe.

He pulled her to him. *No*. Not again. He would be strong this time. He'd fight for them to be together.

Sudden and sharp, desperation infused his blood at the thought of her going back to Canada and them never seeing each other again. Carlos cradled her face in his palms and kissed her.

His fingers tangled in her hair as he pushed his tongue into her mouth.

Carmen moaned, and with only a few steps, he guided her back to the bed.

"We'll make it work," he said in a guttural voice against her neck. "I'm not letting you go again. Never ever again." That was a promise he intended to keep. No way would he let the bitterness from the past ruin the sweet possibilities of the future.

He stripped them of their underwear and joined his body to hers with a swift, hard thrust. Her legs curled around his waist as he rocked back and forth, increasing the tempo until an orgasm pulled whimpering cries from her lips, and he buried his face in her neck, shuddering through his own climax.

13

How am I going to fix this?

Carlos ran a weary hand down his face as he lounged on the gray sofa. Carmen had been gone a couple of days and he was in a slump, missing her the same as if she were an arm or a leg—an integral part of his life whose absence felt painfully unnatural.

She left a message to let him know she landed safely, but they hadn't spoken since, and that was two days ago. It was late, but he needed to talk to her tonight. He sat up and then picked up the phone and dialed her number.

Carmen was sensitive. If she believed you were rejecting her, she'd withdraw so she wouldn't be a nuisance. Though they'd made love before she left, and despite what he'd said, he could imagine her reviewing their intense conversation about Tyler and wondering if Carlos really wanted to be with her.

"Hello?"

He knew she would answer, but still, seeing her face and hearing her voice sent a rush of relief through him. She was lying in bed, hair in a topknot and face make-up-free. He wished he could be there with her among all the linens and pillows, holding her close in his arms.

"Hey," Carlos said.

"Hey," Carmen said.

"I should have called before, but I've been busy with my work. I just called to say I love you."

Her lips smiled, but her eyes held a hint of sadness. "I know. I love you, too, but you don't believe me."

"I do, but I was having a...moment when you were here, that's all. Since then, I've been thinking. You came to see me, and now it's my turn to come see you."

"You're coming here?" Her brown eyes lit up with excitement.

"Yes." Damn, if she didn't make him feel like the grand prize in the most important contest in life. "I'll come in a few weeks, after the Tennessee festival. I'll need to wrap up a few projects, but I should be able to stay in Toronto for a couple of weeks. Then I could go to the other festivals I had planned to attend."

"That would be great, but don't you have to prepare for the events?"

"I do, but I'll be ready for the one in Tennessee, and if need be, I'll skip the other events."

"Carlos, your work is important. I don't want you to do that."

"It's no big deal. I want to see you, and that's all that matters. After I leave Toronto, I'll come back and work hard and see what happens. It'll be fine."

"You're sure?"

"Yes."

"Then you could stay with me!" Her voice pitched higher as her excitement rose.

"I like that idea." He'd planned to stay with his mother, but he liked her idea better.

"Yay," she said softly. She smothered a yawn. "Oops. Sorry."

He chuckled. "You should go to sleep. It's late."

"No, I'm staying up so we can talk."

"But you need to rest. Listen to your body."

She smiled through the biting of her bottom lip. "I'm so glad you're coming. I can't wait. Three weeks!"

He chuckled again. "Three weeks. I have something to take care of, and then I'll start preparing as soon as possible so I can get there like I promised."

"Keep me posted."

"Of course."

"Good night, *mi corazón*."

"Good night, *mi amor*."

She blew him a kiss, and then they both hung up. Carlos rolled onto his back and stared up at the ceiling. He hadn't told Carmen what he needed to take care of, one thing he'd delayed but could no longer avoid. Not if he wanted to be the kind of man she deserved.

He needed to take the first steps toward correcting a decision he now regretted with every fiber of his being.

❧

HE SHOULD HAVE DONE THIS BEFORE, BUT BETTER LATE THAN never.

Carlos restlessly paced the floor outside his financial planner's office at Newmark Advisors. Now that he'd made the decision, the few minutes he waited seemed like forever.

Rashad, his advisor and one of the owners of the company, opened the door of his office. "Come on in, Carlos."

Rashad had dark chocolate skin and was an interesting character whose flamboyant style included a purple and black plaid suit today, which Carlos didn't think anyone else but him could pull off. Despite being a showman and obvious ladies' man, he was one of the nicest guys Carlos had ever met.

Carlos gratefully shook his hand. "Thank you for seeing me on such short notice."

He'd asked Rashad to meet with him immediately, but

because he'd had a full day of appointments, they were meeting during Rashad's lunch hour.

"No problem. Want anything to drink? Or eat—a muffin or a cookie?" Rashad pointed to ice, bottled water, and a platter of muffins and cookies set up on a side table.

"You made those?" Carlos asked.

Another aspect of Rashad's personality that seemed out of place, he liked to bake. Definitely an interesting character.

"Yeah, it's a new recipe I tried. Pistachios and chocolate chips in both. They're not too bad, if I do say so myself."

"Maybe I'll take one of each before I leave."

"Sounds good. Have a seat." Rashad waved to one of the cushioned chairs and sat down behind the desk. He smiled a white-toothed smile that strikingly contrasted with his dark skin and sparkled like the diamonds in each ear. "I've looked into what you asked about."

"And...?" Carlos wanted to take out a loan against his retirement account. "Can it be done?"

"You're not able to take out a loan against any of your accounts."

"I thought that was an option. Why not?" Carlos demanded. He had plenty of money in his portfolio.

Careful and cautious and very frugal, he could afford a nicer and bigger apartment, but he chose a place with low rent and where he could easily get around on foot or by public transportation. That allowed him to put away more money for an uncertain future.

But now he needed some of that money, and Rashad was telling him the opposite of what he'd expected.

"It is an option if your 401K is set up like that, but yours isn't."

"Then I'll just take the money," Carlos said.

Rashad held up a hand. "Wait a minute now, let's not get hasty. If you do that, the money you've already put in is subject to hefty taxes and penalties, so that's not a good idea."

"I'll deal with it," Carlos said grimly. The idea of getting hit with taxes was discouraging, but he intended to forge forward nonetheless.

"There's an alternative, and it's called a solo 401K. It's going to cost you a little bit to set up, but nowhere near what you'd have to pay in taxes for simply pulling out the money. Trust me, it's the better option. You're limited to borrowing up to fifty thousand dollars. Would that work?"

That wasn't the full amount that he needed, but if he emptied his savings, it was a good start.

"I can make it work."

"All right, here are the details."

Rashad handed him some paperwork and launched into an explanation of how he could use the plan to his advantage. When he finished, he sat back and looked at Carlos. "What do you think?"

"Let's do it," Carlos said immediately.

"Great. I know an attorney who can set up the account for you. I'll send you his information, and let's see..." Rashad glanced at his iPad screen. "According to my calendar, I have an opening a week from today, at ten. Can you come back at that time so we can sign some paperwork and get the rollover completed?"

"I'll be here."

"All right, we're all set." Rashad set down the tablet and studied Carlos. "Is everything okay? You're not in any kind of trouble, are you?"

"No. It's...a personal problem I'm hoping to resolve very soon."

Rashad tapped his pen on the desk. "If you need someone to talk to, I'm willing to listen."

"Thanks. I appreciate it, but I can handle this on my own."

Rashad nodded and rose from his chair, signaling the end of the meeting. "I'll see you next week then."

They shook hands. "Thank you, Rashad. You've helped a lot."

"Glad to hear it. Hey, don't forget the cookie and muffin.

Half the people in this office are on diets, and I can't eat them all myself."

Carlos placed a cookie and a muffin on a napkin. "Thanks again."

"Take care."

14

Carmen exited the gym where she'd conducted an inspection as part of her duties. She'd done her job well but was excited about the evening she planned to spend with Carlos. He flew in two days ago, and after they met briefly, he spent two nights at his mother's apartment. Tonight, he was coming to stay at her condo, where he'd remain for the rest of his trip.

She looked forward to each moment they spent with each other as if their relationship was brand new, and in some ways, it was. They were relearning each other because they were different people than they had been three years ago. She saw more confidence in him. He seemed more centered, more focused in a way that calmed her and allowed her to live in the moment without the same level of worry that an outside force could burst their love bubble at any minute.

Carmen stepped into the beaming sunlight and went around to the shaded side of the building where Carlos waited. He was leaning against a rented charcoal SUV in the parking lot, legs crossed at the ankles, eyes trained on the cell phone in his hand.

He must have sensed her presence because he looked up almost immediately, and as he brushed wayward strands of hair back from his face, with one look he softened her knees. She'd been walking since she was eleven months old, but he made the familiar movement harder to execute.

When she almost reached him, he pushed off the vehicle and took several steps forward and enfolded her in his warm embrace.

His hand at her lower back fused her against him, and their lips met in a soft press, slow and sensual. She sipped his flavor, leisurely savoring the sweetness of his mouth—like a particularly tasty piece of candy reserved only for her enjoyment.

When they finally stopped kissing, Carmen sighed and rested her forehead against his chest.

"Tired?" Carlos whispered against her temple.

"No. I just missed you," she replied.

He rubbed a palm up and down her back. "Come on, let's get you home."

But neither of them moved. He must have sensed she needed a moment, so they stood there for several more minutes. Emotion filled her chest, and she knew she couldn't do this much longer.

She couldn't continue to hide her feelings and lie to her family. Carlos was her first love, her last love. Her only love. She wanted to scream those words from the top of the CN Tower, and knowing she'd given him a single moment of doubt made her sick.

He released her and opened the door to the vehicle. She climbed in and watched him walk around to the driver's side. When they were both settled, he started the engine, but Carmen placed a restraining hand on his forearm.

He looked at her. She couldn't read anything more than inquiry in his gaze.

"I'm going to tell my father."

"Carmen, I know you love me. You don't have to do that."

"I want to."

"No. Not yet."

"Why?"

"Because there's so much at stake. He's proud of you right now and all the work you're doing. As far as he's concerned, he has his daughter back. I don't want to be the cause of friction between the two of you."

"You won't be."

He lifted an eyebrow.

"Okay, you will be, but...I don't want to hide our relationship anymore. We did this before, and it didn't work out. I have the perfect plan to set everything in motion. You can escort me to the charity ball I told you about. Beforehand, I'll tell my father you're my escort. I want the world to know that we're together."

Carlos squeezed her hand and brought it to his lips. "They will, but we have to give it time."

"Enough time has passed. Don't you want me to tell him?"

"I do, but..." He looked deeply into her eyes. "I remember what happened before—the rift that our relationship caused in your relationship with your father."

"I'm not a child. I wasn't a child then, and I'm not a child now. I know my own mind, and even though I enjoy the work that I'm doing and the lifestyle I live, I'd walk away from all of it if it meant I couldn't be with you."

He frowned. "You would still do that?"

"Yes," Carmen said emphatically.

"You would live with a starving artist in a one-room loft in Atlanta?"

"You're not a starving artist, but even if you were, I'd still do it and love every minute in that loft with your cat Sofia." She smiled. "I love you. That's all that matters."

Carlos gazed down at their joined hands and rubbed his thumb along the inside of her palm. "I really don't deserve you," he said quietly.

Carmen leaned closer. "Don't ever say that again."

She saw worry in his eyes and hated his doubts.

Carlos cupped her cheek. "Give me—us—a little more time

to enjoy each other. We both know when you tell him about us, unless he's drastically changed his opinion in recent years, the shit will hit the fan. I think we should surprise him the night of the ball."

"I don't know if that's a good idea."

"Warning him ahead of time simply means having to deal with the fallout before the event. Knowing your father, he might ban me from coming." She couldn't argue with him about that. "A surprise is best, especially in a public place, where he'll have to play nice. Not only that, I don't want you talking to him on your own. We should go to him together."

"Okay."

Based on the conversation she overheard in the kitchen between her parents a while back, her father's opinion of Carlos hadn't changed, but she saw no need to mention that. She meant what she said. If her father caused problems for them or demanded she leave Carlos or be cut off, she would walk away. It would hurt not to get his approval and hurt to leave the position at Fit Body Gyms she'd grown to enjoy.

But her love for Carlos was more important than her father's approval or her new-found career.

15

"How do I look?" Carlos straightened the bow tie on his tuxedo.

Carmen came to stand beside him in the mirror. "Handsome. Absolutely perfect."

"And you look amazing." He pressed a soft kiss to her fragrant neck.

He wanted to do much more because she looked so sexy in an ivory, off-the-shoulder dress, but she wouldn't allow him to give her a proper kiss since she didn't want to mess up her makeup. She'd flat-ironed her hair and wore bangs and long, straight extensions that fell to the middle of her back, with diamond drop earrings hanging from her ears.

She leaned against him and slid an arm around his waist. "Thank you." Gazing up at him, she added, "You ready?"

Carlos nodded though about to walk on the emotional equivalent of a bed of nails engulfed in flames, but if that's what it took to have a future with Carmen, he'd gladly walk on a thousand of them. "Yes."

They left the condo together. Franklin, with his customary disapproving stare, opened the door and they climbed in the back. Carmen reached for Carlos's hands as if in an effort to comfort him, but he believed she needed the comfort more than he did based on the nervous half-smile she sent in his direction before they pulled away from the curb.

At the venue, they climbed out of the vehicle, and Carmen's hands tightened on his.

"You okay?" Carlos gazed down at her. She looked like someone about to throw up, and he was doubly glad he hadn't let her talk to Alfred alone. She was so sensitive, and going against her father's wishes was a big step, again. At least this time he was better prepared to deal with the fallout.

Carmen nodded. "Just nervous."

"I'm here." He squeezed her hand, which elicited a faint smile from her lips.

They entered the brightly lit venue, teeming with wealthy guests all ready to whip out their checkbooks and support pee wee soccer, little league baseball, and other sports for less fortunate kids. He didn't like Alfred Reeves one bit, but the man was generous with his money when it came to sports—a passion he'd been forced to give up a long time ago when his professional baseball career ended.

A string quartet played a dulcet tune in the corner, and folks mingled with each other, talking and laughing as if they were old friends. They sauntered through the crowd with Carmen introducing him to some of the executive staff and business associates from other companies. Carlos smiled and shook hands but felt out of place. This wasn't his world, but he needed to relax and accept that a future with Carmen meant attending more events like this, the same way a future with him meant attending art exhibits and festivals. If she could adjust, so could he.

He glanced at her as she engaged in conversation with an older woman and smiled to himself when he realized that he was truly thinking about a future with her. Next steps meant marriage, kids, pets, and living under the same roof, all of which he looked forward to with sudden vigor. But with him living in

Atlanta and her living in Toronto, they had to figure out the logistics of their relationship.

They'd figure it out, because one thing he knew for sure—a future without Carmen was no future at all. The past three years had taught him that.

As the woman walked away, Carmen let out a short breath and scanned the room. "I haven't seen my father yet but knowing him, he's waiting to make an entrance." She lifted two glasses of red wine from a passing waiter's tray and handed one to him.

"That's your second glass of the night," Carlos remarked.

"I know. I'm nervous." She took a sip.

He wished he could ease her mind with soothing words, but her worry came from the fallout years ago, when her father threatened to disown her if she didn't break up with him.

"Nothing to be nervous about. We—"

Carmen stiffened, eyes settled on a point beyond his shoulder. He didn't have to ask what she saw to know her father had made an appearance.

Carlos twisted around and saw Alfred and Graciela Reeves walking toward them. Carmen's uncanny resemblance to her mother still blew him away. The woman had basically given birth to her twin. They were both petite, had generous lips, black hair, and were covered in lovely dark brown skin.

Graciela styled her thick mane in an updo, and she wore a jade-green dress that glittered under the lights. Her eyes widened at the sight of him, but as she approached, a smile split her lips.

"Hello, Carlos. It's been a long time. How are you?" Graciela asked.

"I'm doing well, Mrs. Reeves. And you?"

"Very good. I cannot complain."

"Glad to hear it. Mr. Reeves," Carlos said with a curt nod.

"Carlos, I'm surprised to see you here." Alfred didn't bother with a fake smile or appear friendly in the least.

"Daddy, be nice," Carmen said in a low voice.

"I think a bit of warning would have been appropriate," Alfred said.

"We thought this was better."

"*We* or him?" Alfred said, anger simmering in his eyes.

"Alfred, please." Graciela touched his arm.

Alfred gave a humorless laugh and shoved his hands in the pockets of his tuxedo pants. "You're right, my love. I should behave myself. After all, this is a very nice event, and I wouldn't want to cause any problems. We're going to mingle a little more. You two have a good night." Alfred walked away, and after giving them an apologetic smile, Graciela followed him.

"That went fast and better than expected," Carlos said.

Carmen's eyes followed her parents' movement around the room "He's not done."

Carlos's gut clenched at the ominous tone of her voice. Because he knew she was right.

❧

WHEN CARLOS EXITED THE BATHROOM AND RE-ENTERED THE ballroom, he went in search of Carmen. He strolled the perimeter, eyes scanning for a glimpse of her. The room had filled with more people, and she was so tiny, he didn't see her right away. Finally, he caught sight of her ivory dress as she spoke to a young man near the center of the room.

He took two steps and stopped abruptly when Alfred stepped directly in his path, facing him down with a stony stare.

"Mighty bold of you to come here tonight, considering..."

"That was a long time ago."

"I still want you out of my daughter's life."

Carlos's nostrils flared and his spine stiffened as he quickly surveyed the room to see if anyone paid attention to them. "I can't do that. Accept that fate has brought us back together because we belong together."

"Fate?" Alfred snorted. "You sound ridiculous."

He glared into the eyes of the man who at one time had made him feel inadequate, less than. "Your jabs won't hurt me tonight. I've heard all your remarks, and they no longer make a difference."

"I want you to stay away from her because you're not the right man for her." Alfred smiled and waved at someone nearby. When he returned his attention to Carlos, his face shifted back into hard, unyielding lines. "She can do better than some wannabe artist. Step aside so a man who's worthy of her attention, someone who is an equal, can join her in the life she deserves."

The words bruised his ego, but Carlos refused to back down. "We've had this talk before, remember?"

"And yet here you are."

"Because I love her. Doesn't that mean anything to you?" How could he be so thoroughly heartless when he showered love on his wife and children? His behavior was hard to comprehend.

"Love? Don't make me laugh." Alfred smirked and coolly sipped from his glass of white wine. He was so goddamn condescending.

"Why is that so hard for you to believe?"

"Because men like you take advantage of women like my daughter. I've seen it before. She's trusting and an easy target, and since you have nothing to offer, I'm at a loss as to why she insists on having anything to do with you."

The harsh words smashed a hole in his confidence and were meant to cause doubt, but Carlos fought the urge to succumb to the same insecurities that forced him away from Carmen in the past.

"Don't you get tired of being an asshole?" he asked.

Alfred lifted an eyebrow in surprise. "Finally pushing back against me? What brought that on?"

"Maturity. Growth."

"'Honesty, too? Does she know the kind of man you are?"

"You can't intimidate me like you did before."

"I'd hardly call what I did intimidation." Alfred smirked and drained the last of the wine from his glass.

"I'm not going anywhere. Just accept it and everyone will be happy. I'm in Carmen's life for good."

"You sure about that?" Alfred sent a warning look with direct eye contact.

Carlos straightened his spine, determined not to let this man rattle him. "Take your best shot, Alfred. I'm not going to disappear again. I know what it's like to live without her, and I'm not going back to a life without her in it."

Alfred handed the empty glass to a passing server. With an insolent glance at Carlos, he said, "When you left, you promised you wouldn't move back here."

"I didn't. I live in Atlanta."

A flicker of surprise crossed Alfred's face. "Atlanta? That explains a lot." His mouth pressed together in a grim line.

Shit.

"Did you tell her what you did?" Alfred asked.

Carlos's heart stopped for a split second and let silence be his answer.

"So I take that as a no," Alfred said, with a shake of his head.

"I understand that you don't like me, but have you ever considered Carmen's feelings in this vendetta against me?"

"I'm protecting her—something any decent father would do for his child. My daughter is emotional and impulsive. She can also be rebellious, doing things to get back at me. I simply need to talk some sense into her, but don't worry, Carlos. I won't say a word about your past indiscretion—yet. I'll give you time to think about the consequences and make the right decision."

Alfred walked away, and some time passed before Carlos's muscles relaxed, and only because he saw Carmen approaching.

"Hey. I saw my father talking to you. Is everything okay?" Worried eyes searched his face.

"I'm fine. Everything's fine."

"Are you sure?"

He took her hand to calm her. "I'm not the same nervous kid from three years ago. Your father can't get to me anymore." Not entirely true, but he didn't want her to worry.

She squeezed his hand and gazed up at him with adoration in her eyes.

To look at her, you wouldn't know the burden she carried. The burden of being firstborn but a woman, to a father who wanted her to take over his empire while at the same time believed she couldn't handle the cut-throat life of running a business because she was a woman. The same man wanted her to marry well, not only because he wanted the best for her, but because he didn't think anyone was good enough for his daughter. He couldn't fault him for that. There were many times Carlos didn't think he was good enough for her, either.

"I'm starving. Let's get something to eat," he said.

In the middle of scanning the contents of one of the refreshment tables, Carlos diverted his attention to search the room for Alfred. He saw him and Carmen's mother talking with another couple, and Alfred glanced in his direction. He didn't smile. He didn't nod. He gave no acknowledgement to Carlos except that eye-to-eye contact.

The direct look probably only lasted a few seconds but felt like an eternity before Alfred returned his attention to the conversation.

No doubt about it. Carlos had to tell her everything.

Before her father did.

16

Carmen paused outside the storefront of Azucena's Alpaca Store. The window displayed an array of items—textiles with Inca designs, sweaters, and stuffed alpacas dressed in colorful sweaters or with blankets thrown across their backs. Azucena had achieved her dream, and warm satisfaction brought a smile to Carmen's face. She couldn't be happier for Carlos's mother.

She entered the store, where two customers browsed at a table displaying discounted multi-colored ponchos. Almost immediately, she heard a gasp and turned to see Azucena rushing toward her with arms outstretched.

Carmen happily hugged Carlos's mother, melting into the older woman's warm embrace. Azucena rocked her side to side for a few seconds, moaning her pleasure at finally seeing Carmen again.

When she and Carlos split, she'd cut off contact with his family, too. Not only had it seemed like the right thing to do, the decision mitigated the pain she'd experience if she continued to spend time with them.

Azucena stepped back and shoved her glasses higher on her nose, her dark eyes assessing, her long hair in her customary single braid down her back. With a big, welcoming smile on her face, she asked in her accented voice, "How have you been? You look so beautiful, as usual."

Carmen appreciated the kind words. "I've been well, and I see that you are thriving. Congratulations on opening your own store."

Azucena waved away the compliment. "I could not have done it without Carlos. If it wasn't for him—"

"You're here." Carlos came from the back carrying a large cardboard box in front of him. He rested it on the floor near a display of mittens and scarves. "This is what happens when I come by. She puts me to work."

"Don't listen to him. That's not true. I only sometimes put him to work. I cannot make him work too hard after all he's done for me." Azucena smiled with deep affection at her son.

"Carmen doesn't want to hear about that." Carlos flung an arm around Carmen's shoulders and pulled her closer. "We're going to head out if you don't need anything else...?"

"Nothing else right now, but Carmen, I want you to make me a promise." Azucena took one of Carmen's hands in hers. "You have to come over for dinner one night before Carlos goes back to Atlanta. And of course, you're not limited to visiting when he is here. You are welcome any time."

Carmen squeezed the older woman's hands in hers. "Thank you for saying that. I appreciate it." Considering the way her father had treated Carlos, she'd never been sure about how well she would be welcomed back in the Hortado home. She should have known that Azucena would not hold her father's actions against her. "I'm definitely going to take you up on that dinner offer."

"Good." Azucena patted her hand and gave them both an indulgent smile. "It's good to see you two back together. Have fun."

As they left the store and stepped onto the sidewalk, Carlos tangled his fingers in hers. Walking beside him made Carmen feel as if she were walking on clouds.

"Your mother is still your biggest fan." She gazed up at him.

"I thought you were my biggest fan," he teased.

"Nothing beats a mother as a cheerleader. And what was she talking about, giving you credit for the fact that she was able to open the store?"

"She likes to give me more credit than I deserve. I encouraged her to open the store, and I guess she appreciates it."

Carmen suspected there was more to his mother's comment than what Carlos admitted but knew he wouldn't elaborate, his humble nature keeping him from providing more details.

"Where are we headed?" she asked, as they strolled along the sidewalk.

"I was thinking a board game spot," Carlos replied.

Carmen did a little shimmy. "Woo-hoo! I feel like kicking some butt tonight. Let's do it."

He laughed at her.

"Are you laughing at me or with me?" she asked.

"At you, because you haven't changed. You always talk as if you're the baddest thing to hit board games, but you suck at playing them."

"Oh really? When was the last time you saw me play a game, huh?" she asked.

He thoughtfully frowned at her. "I guess it's been about three years."

"*Exactly*. I assure you, my abilities have improved."

"We'll see about that," Carlos said ominously.

"Yes, we will."

CARLOS HAD TO GIVE CARMEN CREDIT FOR HER BRAGGADOCIO. After three games of Monopoly where Carlos won one game and their opponents won one game each, a hilarious game of Go

Fish, and a particularly sad moment when Carmen failed within three minutes of playing Operation, his suspicions were confirmed. Nothing had change. She still sucked at games.

"I don't know what happened," she said glumly as they left the restaurant.

"Uh-huh."

"I'm serious." She looked so hurt, arms crossed, lips downturned.

Carlos chuckled. "It's okay to suck, *mi amor*." He opened the car, and she glared at him.

"You make me so sick." She climbed into the SUV and slammed the door without waiting for him to close it.

Carlos climbed in the driver's side and closed the door. "How about a kiss," he whispered, leaning closer.

Carmen jerked back. "Nope."

"Come on. Why are you punishing me?"

"Because you're making fun of me and don't believe that I've improved."

"I do believe you. Now can I have a kiss?"

"You're lying."

"Maybe a little bit." He held his forefinger and thumb close together.

She took his hand. "You're not supposed to lie to me. Not even a little bit."

Carlos paused. Her words pricked his conscience, but he hid his reaction. "You're right," he said softly.

"Of course I am. I always am, and you'll do good to remember that," Carmen said haughtily.

"I'll try."

By the time they arrived at her apartment, they were both silent because the reality of him going back to Atlanta the next day loomed before them. They remained silent while they undressed and changed into nightclothes in Carmen's bedroom. Carlos didn't want to say goodbye, but he had to. He also needed to have a serious talk with her. He needed to tell her everything about what he'd done and how sorry he was that he'd done it.

He stuffed folded clothes in his bag on the bed in a disorderly fashion, snapped the suitcase shut, and set it on the floor. Carmen looped her arms around his waist from behind and rested her cheek against his back.

"I don't want you to go," she moaned.

Carlos's shoulders slumped. He didn't want to leave, either, and the burden of keeping the secret from her ate at him even more. He should tell her now, but the timing didn't feel right, and his heavy heart needed a pick-me-up. He needed her and her love for a little bit longer, because everything would change once he opened up.

He turned and pulled her into his embrace. "I don't want to go, either." Weeks, possibly months, would pass before they saw each other again.

Carmen sighed. "I wish..."

"You wish what?"

She shrugged. "Nothing."

"Tell me," Carlos said.

She swallowed. "I'm not trying to make you feel guilty or influence you in any way, but...I wish we could live in the same city. Have you ever considered moving back to Toronto?" She asked the question tentatively.

"I've thought about it a lot since you and I reconnected."

"So it's a possibility? I know you've established yourself in Atlanta, but...being away from you is so hard."

"Being away from you is harder." He folded her in his arms and sighed. "Let me think about it and see what I can do, okay?"

"Okay." Carmen shifted her hands underneath his shirt and caressed his sides and back. Nothing felt as good as her soft hands on his skin.

He kissed her deeply and thoroughly as he pushed the panties down her hips and then lifted her onto the bed. Her nipples tightened against his chest as she wrapped her arms around his torso and welcomed him on top of her and then finally inside of her soft, wet body.

***

Something was wrong.

As Carmen slowly woke up, she realized what was wrong. Carlos was not in bed with her. She flicked on the bedside lamp and squinted as her eyes adjusted to the light. Her ears picked up what sounded like talking. She raised up on her elbows and tilted her head to hear better but couldn't discern any words—only the low murmur of Carlos's voice.

She slid off the mattress, slipped on the nightshirt that had been discarded when they made love earlier, and tiptoed to the door. She heard him better now, and he sounded agitated, frustrated.

Easing open the door, she winced, hoping the hinges didn't make a sound. Luckily, they didn't. She peered out and saw Carlos at the far end of the living room, his muscular body mostly a shadow against the curtained windows.

"No, I don't have all of the money right now. I—" He paused. Even in the darkness, she saw the taut way he held his body as he listened to the person on the other end of the line.

A thread of unease filtered into her sleep-addled brain and made her more alert. Who was he talking to?

"Tell me how much interest you want." Pause. "You're being unreasonable. Just give me a... Why are you doing this?"

The rest of the words were cut off as he dropped his voice into an even fiercer whisper, shoulders rounded as he hunched over the phone. Steeped in worry, Carmen took a step into the room, ears straining to hear. She thought she'd been quiet but wasn't as quiet as she should have been because Carlos swung in her direction.

She stared at him in the darkness. She couldn't see his

features, but considering the circumstances, she sensed he was not pleased to see her standing there.

"I have to go," he said in a clipped voice. He ended the call. "What are you doing up?" He walked slowly toward her.

"I heard talking."

"What did you hear?" He stood in front of her now, and she clearly saw the remnants of anger from the conversation, but concern, too. The concern had to be because she'd learned something about him that he didn't want her to know.

"Sounds like you owe someone money," Carmen said quietly.

"It's my problem," he muttered and swept past her back to the bedroom.

She followed close on his heels. "So you're keeping things from me?"

"Not exactly. This is something I need to handle on my own." Carlos set the phone on the nightstand and sat on the edge of the bed. He ran his fingers through his hair.

Carmen walked over and stroked her fingers over his furrowed brow. The creases cleared, but his eyes remained troubled.

"I don't like this. Who were you talking to? That conversation sounded really intense, and whatever you're going through, I want to help."

"I can't tell you anything except that I'll handle the problem, and there's nothing for you to worry about. The conversation may have sounded intense, but I have everything under control. And I don't need your money. The last thing I want to do is take money from you for problems I created myself."

"So you admit there's a problem. Carlos—"

"Carmen, listen to me." He took both of her hands and tugged her forward until she stood between his legs. "You have to trust me right now, okay? I know I seem very secretive, but it's for a good reason. You can't help me, and I can handle this on my own."

She stared down at the hands grasping hers.

"Hey." He tugged more gently this time and forced her eyes to focus on his. "Stop worrying."

"If you need my help, you would tell me, right?"

"Yes. But this is something I need to take care of myself. I can't explain, and I won't let you help me."

"Please don't let your stupid male pride create problems when I'm right here and able to assist," she pleaded.

"It's not male pride. It's me trying to right a wrong. An error in judgment that I regret."

"Doesn't sound like the person you were talking to will allow you to fix it."

"Not right now, but I'm working on the situation, and I need time, that's all." He squeezed her hands. "Trust me. This problem is nothing you need to concern yourself with."

She straddled his thighs and wound her arms around his neck. "I accept your answer. I don't like it, but I do, because I trust you. I only have one question, and I need you to answer me honestly. Are you involved in anything illegal?" She hated to ask, but a late-night, furtive conversation that he couldn't give her details about had her imagination running wild.

He actually graced her with a brief smile. "Nothing quite so exciting."

Carmen breathed a little easier. "Good. Then I'll leave it alone, and you can tell me when you're ready."

Carlos kissed her softly and tightened his arms around her waist. "Thank you for trusting me."

"Don't make me regret it."

For two seconds, his brow creased again, but then the lines disappeared. "I'll do my best," he said solemnly, which was not the answer she'd wanted to hear.

17

Carmen walked through the halls of Fit Body Gyms corporate office with an extra pep in her step. Tomorrow she'd be on a plane to Atlanta. A month had passed since she last saw Carlos in the flesh, and she couldn't wait to be with him again.

She stopped at her assistant's desk, Trudy, an older redhead with black-framed glasses whose sunny disposition always brightened her day.

"Almost ready to leave?" Trudy asked with a knowing grin.

Carmen had confided in her about Carlos and explained that they'd reunited, without divulging Alfred's role in the split. She didn't want to sully her father's reputation. After all, he was still the head of the company and came in every day. No need to start gossip that would cause employees to dislike him.

"Almost. Before I do, I need twenty copies each of these and the Mathis contract emailed to me so I can work on the revisions. I'm going to take it home with me tonight."

"Will you have time to read it, with packing and getting ready to leave tomorrow?" Trudy asked.

"I had Valencia pack for me," Carmen replied, referring to

her housekeeper. She handed over the papers to Trudy. "But even if she hadn't, I'd stay up all night because I'm determined to complete the revisions and have the final copy ready before I leave." The last thing she wanted was to let her personal travels affect her work.

"Now that's dedication, or someone determined not to let work interrupt their trip," Trudy said.

Carmen laughed, downright giddy she would soon be able to see Carlos. "A little bit of both, but I'll be working in Atlanta like I always do. This isn't a vacation. I just need to get that contract completed and in to legal by first thing Monday morning."

Carmen headed toward her office.

"You'll be missed around here for the next week," Trudy called after her. "By the way, your father stopped by while you were in the meeting."

Carmen turned away from the door. "Did he say what he wanted?"

Trudy adjusted the glasses on her nose. "Only that I should let you know he stopped by and that it was important that he speak to you."

"Thanks. Could you order me something from the Japanese place? The usual. I'm going to eat lunch at my desk." She could go through emails while eating, crossing one more item off her list of things to do today.

"Got it," Trudy said, already picking up the phone.

Carmen closed the door to her office and sank into the leather chair. Frowning, she considered picking up the phone and finding out what her father wanted but doubted it was anything important. They'd barely spoken since Carlos went back to Atlanta because he'd let his reservations about their relationship be known yet again.

To avoid confrontation, she stayed away from her parents' house and steered clear of her father at work, which wasn't that hard to do since they were both often quite busy. She could count on one hand how many times they'd spoken since the night at the charity event, and all conversations had been brief.

She'd waited until the last minute to mention her trip to Atlanta, and now he clearly wanted to corner her and give her another talking to. Well, she wasn't interested. He'd simply have to deal with his own negativity. It wasn't her problem.

SITTING WITH HER LEGS CROSSED AT THE ANKLES AND PROPPED on top of the coffee table, Carmen munched on popcorn as she reviewed the contract on her lap. Using a blue-ink pen, she made notes in the margin and rewrote sentences that she crossed out.

Two firm knocks on the door dragged her out of deep concentration. Only one person knocked like that, and only one person would dare to come to her home after nine o'clock, unannounced. Sighing, she set aside the document and dusted her hand on her sweats.

She didn't bother to check the peep hole. She opened the door and wasn't remotely surprised to see her father standing in the hallway.

"Do you mind if I come in?" Alfred asked.

Carmen walked away without greeting him, at the point now where she no longer cared. If he gave her an ultimatum, she knew what her answer would be.

She stood in the middle of the living room with her arms crossed. "Whatever you have to say, say it and leave." No point in beating around the bush with pleasantries. They both knew why he was there.

"Is that any way to talk to your father?" He still wore a suit, which meant he had stayed late at the office and come here before going home.

"Daddy I love you, but you've made me this way. You never have anything good to say about Carlos, and I know this so-called important conversation is about him, and I don't want to hear you bad-mouth him anymore. Three years have passed, he's successful as an artist and is working at becoming more successful. He may never be wealthy like we are, but he makes an honest living. Why isn't that enough?"

Alfred sighed as if she exhausted him. "When you have children, you'll understand. I had different expectations for you. I worked my fingers to the bone so you could have everything I didn't have growing up. I didn't do all that so you could throw it away on some artist with a pipe dream, Carmen."

"Being with Carlos doesn't mean I'm throwing away my livelihood. This is the same spiel you've always given me. Nothing has changed."

"You're only twenty-five years old. Why don't you wait a while before you make any major decisions?"

"You weren't worried about my age when you tried to set me up with Tyler."

His jaw hardened. "Fair enough. But in my defense, he's a much better prospect. The kind of man who has his own money and wouldn't be using you for a financial windfall."

"You're being ridiculous."

"This boy has turned you against me."

"No, he hasn't! Your actions have made me this way." Her heart ached. "Why are you like this?"

"You know why I'm like this!" Alfred said with vehemence. "You know how that guy used my sister, milking her for money every chance he got. If my father and I hadn't stepped in, who knows where she would be right now. Thank goodness she finally came to her senses. And what about that fool you met at the mall, huh? Soon as you were allowed to date, you got caught up with some ne'er-do-well with no money. That boy had you buying him shoes!" He sounded appalled.

"It was one pair of shoes." He'd mentioned the shoes, and she'd surprised him with them.

"And you paid for your dates."

"Only a few times!"

"Hah. Trust me, it was just the beginning." Alfred pinched his nose. "I want to take care of you, Carmen. You're my daughter. That's what fathers do—we take care of our kids. It's what my father did. You can't fault me for loving you."

She sighed and swallowed. It pained her to be at odds with her father. "No, I don't," she said, softening her voice. "But I fault you for treating the man I love like he's unwelcomed. You're hurting me by doing that. Carlos and I are in love with each other. My feelings for him haven't changed in all this time, and his for me haven't changed. I wish you would accept our relationship and give your blessing. Welcome him instead of making this so hard." Her voice trembled at the end.

Alfred studied her. "I know better than you what kind of man he is."

Carmen shook her head. "No, you don't. I know what kind of man he is. He's kind, and he loves me. He left before because of you. Don't chase him away again. Please. Because if you do, this time I'm going with him, and you won't see me again."

Alarm entered Alfred's eyes. "You don't mean that."

"I meant it before. I didn't leave because...because Carlos wanted to go alone. He was worried he couldn't take care of me. But this time, nothing will keep us apart."

"Is that what he told you? That he was worried he couldn't take care of you?"

"Yes."

Alfred chuckled and shook his head. "And you think you know him?"

His smug response sounded as if he knew something she didn't, which made Carmen frown. "I *do* know him."

"You don't know him like I do. You don't know the kind of man he is," Alfred said. "I didn't want to hurt you, but he's left me no choice. *You* have left me no choice."

The pit of her stomach contracted in fear, and her bluster took a hit. "What are you talking about?"

"He didn't tell you about the money, did he?"

"What money?"

Alfred sighed and sat down. He patted the cushion beside him. "Have a seat, and I'll tell you everything."

18

Carlos checked the time and then flipped the plant-based burgers on the stovetop grill. He and Carmen had discussed going meatless two days this week. He'd tried this brand of patties before, and they were pretty tasty. He figured Carmen would like them, too.

"She'll be here soon, Sofia," he said to the cat, who lapped water from her bowl nearby. For some reason, Carmen was bringing Franklin with her this time, and he would bring her to the apartment.

Carlos double-checked the contents of the refrigerator and then sprayed air freshener throughout the loft. When he finished, he removed each burger, set them on plates, and covered them with foil to keep them warm. Several minutes later, while slicing tomatoes, the doorbell rang.

"Shit," he muttered. He'd hoped to have everything ready before she arrived.

He set down the knife and went to the door. When he saw Carmen, as lovely as ever in a pair of thigh-hugging jeans and a white cashmere sweater, he became overwhelmed. Damn, he loved this woman. She was standing on his doorstep, and they'd have an entire week together. He needed to figure out how to move back to Canada because the time they spent apart was eating away at his soul.

Carlos immediately swept her up in his arms, burying his face in her rose-scented hair. "*Mi amor*, it's so good to see you."

He set her on her feet and moved to kiss her, but oddly enough, she dodged his lips.

Startled, Carlos stared for a second but held on to her arms. "Hey, something wrong?" He glanced behind her. "Franklin didn't bring up your bags?"

Carmen eased away from him and shut the door. "They're downstairs."

That was strange. Why didn't Franklin just bring them up?

"Do you need me to go down and get them?" Carlos asked.

She'd told him not to come to the airport to pick her up because she was bringing Franklin with her and he'd make sure she got here, but maybe she was upset he hadn't pushed harder. He couldn't read her mood. He expected her to be as happy to see him as he was to see her, but instead, she appeared cool—almost aloof so far.

"No." Carmen rubbed her hands together and walked around him and farther into the apartment.

"I made veggie burgers. I'm almost done with the fixings."

Carmen turned and the emotion in her eyes rooted him to the spot. A deep sadness filled their depths, and he almost dragged her back into his arms again. "What's wrong?"

She blinked rapidly. "Since last night, I've been trying to figure out how to broach this topic with you. I even considered not coming, but I thought...no, that was a bad idea. Because I said I was coming, and I wanted to do this face to face. And I wanted to give you a chance to explain because maybe my father was wrong or had lied." She swallowed hard.

Carlos waited for the inevitable bomb to drop.

"Did you take money from my father to leave me?" Carmen whispered shakily.

His heart stopped. Carlos wanted to sink into the earth. His time was up. A glimmer of tears sat in Carmen's eyes, while the twist of remorse bored a hole in his conscience.

"I can explain," he said.

Her mouth fell open, as if she'd expected him to deny the accusation. He wished he could. Three years ago, he and Alfred had agreed to keep their transaction a secret, but Alfred had warned at the charity event that he'd tell her now that Carlos was back in her life. Carlos had intended to come clean about the money himself, but he'd thought he had more time.

"It's true?" she whispered. "You took money from my father?"

He walked toward her. "It's not what you think."

Carmen jerked away and held up both hands. "Don't touch me," she said in a thick voice, shaking her head in disbelief. "You walked away...for money? That's how you have all this?" She spun in a circle and then faced him again, eyes wide, mouth still agape.

Carlos licked his lips. "I didn't want to leave," he said, in the calmest, quietest voice he could.

She laughed and stared up at the ceiling, blinking rapidly. When her gaze landed on him again, the tears of disbelief were gone and a wounded expression filled her eyes. "The money was too tempting, is that it? He made you an offer you couldn't refuse? I was going to walk away from *everything* for you. Millions. My inheritance."

Like lashes, her words burned through his skin.

"How much did my father pay you?" she asked.

Carlos hung his head. They couldn't be having this conversation. Not after he'd won her back and come to a decision on how to fix his huge mistake. He wanted her permanently back in his life. This couldn't be happening right now.

"Carmen..."

"How much was breaking my heart worth to you, Carlos?" she asked.

"It wasn't like that. It wasn't about the money."

"Answer me. Or I can always ask my father. That was the one

bit of information he refused to divulge, but he promised to tell me if you wouldn't."

Quiet filled the loft, and he turned the answer over and over in his mind, wishing for a way to avoid giving her an answer.

"Two hundred thousand," Carlos replied, almost choking on the words.

She shook her head in a pitying way. "You went too cheap. You could have negotiated more. Or maybe it didn't matter. You got what you wanted, right?"

The money had been unexpected good fortune for his family —a raft in the middle of the sinking ship of their lives. That amount wasn't much to her, but it had done a lot of good. Paid off bills, helped his mother open a business, and provided financial assistance to family back in Peru.

He shuffled closer but didn't dare touch her. "I wanted you. I just..." He didn't know what to say. Nothing excused what he did.

He had assumed Carmen would forget about him and find the right kind of man eventually. One who didn't see the money, no matter how meagre in her eyes, as an opportunity to help his family. One who wouldn't take money from a man who despised him. He swallowed the nasty taste of regret.

"My dad was right about you."

"No, he wasn't. I love you. Please, you have to believe me. I'm sorry for what I did. It was a mistake, but I loved you, Carmen. I still do."

"Then why'd you take the money?" she asked in a voice thick with tears. Her eyes became wet again.

"I don't know. Desperation. Do you think I wanted to take his money? I felt I didn't have a choice. I couldn't give you the life you deserved, so I thought...maybe I could do something else. I helped my mother get her business started, and...and..."

"And you helped yourself. Good for you. You did what was best for you and your family, and that's what's most important. Self. Family."

He shook his head. "I barely kept any of it. Only enough to

get me here to get started, that's it. Every other dime went to family in Canada and in Peru." He knew where the conversation was headed, and he didn't want to hear her say they were finished.

"Thank you for your honesty, Carlos. Goodbye. For good this time." She gave him wide berth as she rushed to the door.

"Carmen!"

They reached the door at the same time. As she yanked it open, he slammed his palm beside her head, shutting it again.

She swung around, eyes blazing with fury. "Let me go."

He brought his face closer to hers. "Not again. *Never* again."

"Why? Because you won't be compensated this time? That can be arranged."

"I'm not a heartless, greedy monster. I didn't use you for money. It *killed* me to leave without you. Don't do this. Don't make what we have now—"

"*We don't have anything.*"

Her words drove a stake in his heart, and for several seconds he couldn't speak, the wound so deep and debilitating.

Finally, he found the words. "I love you. I would give it all back if I could, with interest—"

"I don't care!"

"—to not have you look at me like this. I've tried several times, but he won't take it."

"I don't care! Move your hand!" she screamed.

Carlos's voice grew louder too. "That's who you heard me arguing with that night. He said we had a deal. He won't take the damn money!" His breath came in short, pained spurts.

As soon as he'd set up the solo 401K, he called Alfred and made an offer of a large down payment to reimburse him. He refused the payment. Carlos tried again after their conversation at the charity ball. Again her father rebuffed him.

Carmen's bottom lip trembled, and she ducked her head.

"Carmen," he whispered. "*Por favor, mi amor.*"

She gave her head a vigorous shake and then glared at him, as if his words had angered her. "I am not your love, and you are not my heart. I know the truth now, and I can't un-know. Let. Me. Go."

Carlos's flat palm turned into a fist against the door. Should he let her leave or hold her hostage until she listened and accepted that he'd made a terrible mistake? Maybe it was better to let her go now. Later they could talk, without the emotion, when she was calmer and willing to listen.

"Where are you going?"

"None of your damn business."

He swallowed and then stepped back.

She took a deep breath and then turned, opened the door, and closed it without another word. Carlos stared at the cold metal, his thoughts swirling in a dizzying array of doubt. Had he made the right decision? Should he have tried harder? Would she be lost to him forever now?

Seized by panic, he swung open the door.

He saw no sign of her but called out anyway. "Carmen, wait!" His voice echoed in the hallway, and he hurried toward the staircase, barefoot and determined to stop her. He caught a glimpse of her at the bottom of the stairs before she disappeared.

"Carmen!"

Grabbing on to the railing on either side, he hopped down the stairs, three at a time.

As he pushed through the door, she dived into the waiting Lincoln Navigator and Franklin shut the door. Carlos ran forward, but the big man stepped in front of him, arms crossed, staring down through his dark aviator sunglasses. An impenetrable mahogany wall. Carlos pulled up short, staring helplessly at the tinted windows which he couldn't see beyond.

"That's as far as you go," Franklin said.

"Carmen, hear me out!" Carlos yelled.

A woman riding by on a bike stared at them.

He shouldn't have let her go. He should have locked her in the apartment and begged and pleaded until she forgave him.

She couldn't leave like this, doubting his love for her. Believing he'd preferred the money over her. He'd simply thought he had no choice, but looking back, he did have a choice. He could have chosen her, and he didn't. The biggest regret of his life.

Franklin didn't budge, and he wouldn't. He'd probably die trying to keep Carlos away from her. Now he knew why she'd brought him this time.

His fingers curled into his palms, and Franklin's face transformed into stone when he saw Carlos's fists.

"I wouldn't if I were you," he warned.

With deep regret, Carlos backed away from the vehicle, but Franklin remained in position, still watching him. When he decided that Carlos had moved far enough away, he opened the door and slid into the driver's seat.

Carlos heard the power locks engage on the inside.

Seconds later, the vehicle pulled away, leaving him alone on the sidewalk.

19

Carlos hung up the phone in frustration and tossed it on the sofa. Restlessly, he paced the floor.

Where was she? She could at least respond to let him know she received the half a dozen texts and four voicemails he'd left in the few hours since she'd been gone. Had she left for the airport or was she still in the city? He couldn't stay here. Wondering. Waiting. He'd go mad.

Carlos stopped pacing. Natalie! If Carmen hadn't gone to the airport, she was probably at Natalie's.

He grabbed his keys and raced out of the apartment. He drove over the speed limit to Natalie's place and parked in the underground parking lot. Since he couldn't get upstairs without being buzzed in, he waited outside her building. At some point, one of the tenants would come out or go in, and then he could slip inside and plead his case from outside the apartment door.

Lucky for him, mere minutes later, Natalie exited the building with earbuds tucked into her ears. She hadn't noticed him against the outer wall. The same thick twists cascaded down her back as she bounced down the sidewalk to the tune in her ears.

Carlos walked up behind her and tapped her on the shoulder. "Natalie."

She spun around, and when she saw him, her face transformed into a scowl. She removed the buds, and he heard the faint sound of a hip-hop track. "What do you want?"

This was going to be very, very hard. "I need to talk to Carmen. I need to see her."

"No and no. She doesn't want to talk to you or see you. You've done enough."

He fought the urge to yell in anger. "I need to explain the situation."

Natalie smiled sweetly—too sweetly. Tilting her head, she blinked up at him. "From what I hear, you already explained. There's nothing more for you to say. Carmen knows what you did and why you did it, and she doesn't care. You were wrong, and apologizing isn't going to change that. Leave her alone."

"I can't."

"Why not? You did before, with your pockets full of cash."

Carlos winced, and she looked almost apologetic.

"I love her."

"If that's true, then you shouldn't want to hurt her," Natalie said.

"I don't. I didn't. I made a mistake. She loves me, Natalie. Let me inside the apartment to talk to her. I only need five minutes."

"I am not going to betray her trust for you. Carmen is a good person, a sweetheart. Her heart broke when you left, and now to find out your absence was *bought*...how do you think that makes her feel?"

Her words and unyielding stance revealed the hopelessness of the situation.

"She didn't deserve what you did. Let her be, Carlos." Natalie tucked the buds back in her ears and walked away.

Carlos shifted his gaze up the side of the building to the

windows above. Carmen was up there. She might even be looking at him right now. So close, yet so far away.

He dropped his gaze to the street filled with cars and shoppers and inhabitants of the buildings, and emptiness filled him. They were supposed to be spending the week together.

Taking her father's money had been an act of desperation—one he wasn't proud of—and one he couldn't explain without a deep sense of shame and regret. Regret that he'd lost Carmen, and now he was losing her all over again.

Gulping back his pain, he put one foot in front of the other and walked slowly back to his car.

❧

CARMEN STARED UP AT THE CEILING IN HER OLD BEDROOM AT her parents' house, having sought refuge here upon her return to Toronto a few days ago. She hadn't seen her father because he was out of town. She wasn't sure what she would say to him when he did arrive because she'd been so ugly to him and so rude during their last face-to-face conversation, when he truly had only been trying to protect her. She'd called him a liar, but in reality, he knew Carlos's true character.

A knock sounded on the door, and she rolled her head to the side and called, "Come in."

Her mother walked in with a steaming cup and a sympathetic expression on her face. Carmen sat up against the pillows and accepted the chamomile tea.

Graciela sat on the side of the bed and watched as Carmen took a sip and then rested the cup and saucer on the bedside table.

"How are you feeling, *mija*?" she asked.

"The same." Carmen shrugged.

She might never return to the optimistic, easy-going person she used to be. She was disillusioned, hurt, and saddened not only by

Carlos's decision, but also by her own inability to see him for who he really was. Was she so blinded by the romanticism of falling in love and her parents' example of a happy marriage that she had been willing to accept anything? Willing to turn a blind eye to Carlos's true character? Even now, she couldn't remember a moment in their relationship—past or present—when he had ever treated her less than respectfully or lovingly. He was simply that good at faking his feelings for her. Sadly, she had been right all along. She loved him more than he loved her. In fact, he'd clearly never loved her at all.

"I'm so sorry," Graciela said.

"I'll be fine...eventually."

Carmen knew from experience that this feeling of loss would not easily disappear. She should have listened to Natalie—managed her expectations and taken things slow.

She had left Atlanta, a city where the metropolitan area included millions of inhabitants, because it had not been big enough for her to avoid thoughts of Carlos. Particularly since he had been so relentless in trying to reach her, going so far as to come to Natalie's apartment the same day that she had confronted him about the money.

In her heart of hearts, she still wanted a future with him. Now that the anger had passed, longing had taken its place. Maybe there was something wrong with her, but she'd always been the type who loved hard.

She still felt Carlos everywhere. So ridding him from her mind would be difficult. She couldn't face going home yet because he had spent time at her apartment, and the memories of them laughing together and making love tormented her too much. He had left a mark in every aspect of her life, simply by being.

"You should not be going through this. Your father loves you and wants the best for you, and usually I don't interfere in his decisions. But if I had known what he planned to do, I would have stopped him. I see how much this hurts you, and it's not right. He was wrong for what he did."

"No, actually, he was right. No matter how much I hate what he did, in his own twisted way, he proved what he had been saying all along about Carlos. He only cared about the money and what he could financially get out of our relationship. As soon as Daddy offered him money, he disappeared. He left the country to pursue his dreams and live a life without me in it. He didn't care about *me*." Her voice cracked at the end.

"I don't believe that," Graciela said.

A tear slipped from the corner of Carmen's eye and slid down the side of her nose. Angrily, she wiped it away. She had thought she was done crying, but it seemed the tears would never end.

Graciela took her hand. "You might not be ready to hear these words yet, but I saw how Carlos looked at you. He looked at you the way Alfred used to and still looks at me—with nothing but love and adoration in his eyes. He made the wrong decision, yes, but I don't doubt that he loved you. I believe the decision to accept the money was an act of desperation."

Her mother was correct—she wasn't in the right frame of mind to listen to an argument in favor of Carlos. Not with such fresh, deep wounds. Not when he'd had every opportunity to tell the truth but had chosen not to.

"You and Carlos belong together," her mother said quietly. "Go be with your young man. I'll deal with your father." Her last sentence held a steely note.

Carmen shook her head. She looked at her mother, grateful for the words she spoke but knowing they made no difference. "I can't go to him. I don't believe in him anymore."

He had broken her heart twice, and she would not give him the opportunity to do so a third time.

❧

"THANKS FOR SEEING ME." CARLOS ENTERED RASHAD'S OFFICE.

The flamboyant financial planner wore a purple suit today

and the usual diamond earrings in his ears. By the way he eyed Carlos, he probably looked like a big mess, the way he felt.

Carlos hadn't shaved in days and had barely slept during that same period. Yesterday, after two weeks, he finally gave up calling and texting Carmen. She hadn't responded to any of his messages—verbal or written—or to the flowers he'd sent, and she'd blocked his number.

"Not a problem. You didn't sound good, so I knew the situation was serious. Besides, I meant what I said when I told you that you could come to me if you ever needed someone to talk to." The chair squeaked as Rashad laid his arms on the rests and leaned back, waiting for Carlos to proceed.

Carlos dropped onto the chair opposite Rashad, weary with the burden of his thoughts and the inability to fix the mess his relationship with Carmen had become. He couldn't accept that it was over.

He launched into an explanation of their meeting and courtship, as well as their break-up three years go. Shamefaced, he explained about the money he'd accepted from Alfred, recounted the argument in his apartment that made Carmen leave, and ended with the torture of no contact the past two weeks. When he finished, he sat quietly and waited.

Rashad had listened as he talked, nodding every now and again but overall not revealing any emotion or judgment in his expressions.

"Well, now I understand why you wanted the money from your retirement account so badly."

Carlos nodded and ran fingers through his rumpled curls. "In a nutshell. For the past couple of weeks, I've felt as if my life is at a standstill. I'm still going through the motions—painting, eating, drinking, sleeping when I'm able. But that's all they are—motions. I don't *feel* anything. Nothing gives me joy."

If he could, he'd stay in bed all day every day, but he had obligations. He had a commissioned piece to complete, but he'd already asked for an extension and pushed back the date of delivery.

"Since she blocked my number, I tried calling her at work, but I can't get through there, either. She's completely cut me off."

He thought about enlisting his mother to get a message to Carmen but changed his mind. He didn't want to get her involved, and further, he didn't want her to feel guilty. He never told her where he got the money to help her open the store, send money back home to family, and get himself out of Toronto. He hinted that it had come from a wealthy benefactor, and that alone made her feel bad that maybe she'd taken money from him that he'd earned.

But he hadn't earned a dime of it. The funds were tarnished, which was why he hadn't had the heart to keep but a small portion. At the time, it had seemed like so much money. Life-changing—and it had been. In more ways than one.

Rashad sat forward and folded his hands together on the desktop. "Listen, I don't know Carmen, but it sounds like you really love this woman. My question to you is, what are you willing to do to get her back? From what you've told me, calling and texting ain't working."

"I'm willing to do anything. I'm willing to lose everything. More than everything, to have her back in my life."

Rashad sat back with a smile befitting an ancient wise man. "Then maybe that's your answer."

20

Carmen straightened the shawl around her shoulders against the chilly air. She'd hoped the night out would lift her spirits, but the opposite had happened. The show and dinner only reminded her of how much she missed Carlos because she wished she'd attended both of them with him.

She strolled toward the front of the building and stopped ten feet away, turning to face her date. Tyler stopped too. He looked questioningly into her face. He was handsome, with thick lips and almost flawless skin the color of cream-diluted coffee. Why couldn't she feel anything more for him?

"This is it, isn't it?" A wry smile lifted the corner of his mouth.

"I'm sorry. I just... My heart isn't in it."

He nodded. "I figured as much. You seemed distracted tonight, and after you explained the situation to me about your break-up with Carlos, I wondered if you were ready to start dating again. I see that you're not."

She hadn't told him about Carlos taking the money, but she had told him that they had reunited and then broken up again.

"I'm not," she admitted with regret.

"This is the part where you tell me it's not me, it's you. And that I'll make some other woman a great boyfriend."

She laughed, one of the first real laughs she'd had all night. "Do I really need to do that if you already know what needs to be said?"

"True. We'll pretend you said all of that, and I will go on my way, gracefully." He pulled her into a friendly hug and kissed her right cheek. "Just because we don't work as a couple doesn't mean we can't be friends. Hopefully that guy Carlos will get his act together and treat you the way you deserve."

"He and I are done for good."

Tyler studied her for a couple of beats. "Nah, I don't think so. Good night, Carmen."

"Good night, Tyler."

She watched him walk away and then waved her card at the electronic keypad, and the doors slid apart to allow her in. She had gone only a short distance into the interior when she heard a male voice behind her.

"Back with Tyler?"

Not believing her ears, Carmen did a one-eighty spin and gasped when she saw Carlos. He'd slipped in behind her.

Her heart constricted at the sight of him in a white shirt with the sleeves rolled up, black pants, and shiny black shoes. His long hair was neatly pulled back away from his face, and his features—the large nose, warm brown eyes, and olive-toned skin were so achingly familiar she wanted nothing less than to throw herself into his arms and sob with relief that he was there.

But what good would that do? Nothing had changed. He was still a liar. He'd still taken money to break her heart. But she had her doubts. Had she been too hard on him? Two hundred thousand dollars had been life-changing for the Hortados.

"What are you doing here?"

"I came to see you because you wouldn't take my calls and blocked my number. Are you back with him?" Tension reeked from his pores.

"No. And for the record, I was never with him before." Carmen straightened, firming her resolve with the firming of her spine. "You should go."

"Not before I've said what I came to say. Not before I tell you how much I love you and how sorry I am for what I did."

"Forget about me."

"I can't. There's no way I could forget about you unless someone wipes my memory clean."

"Empty words that don't mean anything. Love means *nothing* to you. You don't understand the concept of love and sacrifice. Or maybe you do, but you don't care. Either way, I'm not interested in anything you have to say. I suggest you fly back to Atlanta because you wasted your time coming here."

Stay strong. Be hard. Don't give in.

"I can't go back to Atlanta," Carlos said in a low tone.

"Am I supposed to ask why not?" A heavy dose of sarcasm rested in her voice.

"I don't have anything to go back to."

"What does that even mean?"

"My whole life is here now. I sold my car and broke the lease on the loft. I finished up my painting obligations, and then I sold or gave away the majority of my belongings. Sofia and I moved here, to Toronto. I'm staying at my mother's until I find an apartment and can get back on my feet."

"Wh...I..." Had she misunderstood? "Why would you do that?"

"Because I plan to win you back. You're the most important thing in my life. Nothing matters without you in it."

"So you walked away from your whole life?" she asked, aghast.

"Yes."

"That's ridiculous and crazy. It doesn't make sense." He'd had to build up a reputation in the art community, which had taken years to establish. He'd almost have to start all over.

"You were willing to walk away from your whole life for me."

The gravity of his words hung in the air between them.

Carmen swallowed the lump in her throat. "Your decision to move here doesn't change anything."

"I know I still have work to do, but I wanted you to know. I'm serious, and I'm not giving up. I'm doing what I should have done back then. Trusted in us. Been willing to sacrifice."

"But then your mother wouldn't have her shop." Despite her dismay at what he'd done, she could acknowledge that he'd used the money to benefit his family's financial position and helped create a business that not only benefited his siblings, but was a potential inheritance for them.

"We could have found another way. I'm here, and I'm not leaving. I love you, Carmen, and I'm going to prove it, and I'm going to make you love me again."

At the end, his voice became husky with emotion, and she had to look away as tears welled in her eyes unexpectedly. The elevator doors opened and a couple came out.

"Hi, Carmen," the man and woman said in unison, casting curious eyes at Carlos.

She smiled faintly at them because she couldn't speak. When they'd walked through the door, she ventured a look at Carlos.

"I meant every word," he said in a solemn tone.

"We'll see how serious you are." Carmen's hands tightened in the soft material of the shawl.

"We will. Good night, *mi universo*," Carlos said softly.

He turned around, and a dizzying burst of panic seized Carmen. "Wait!" she said in a trembling voice.

Carlos turned to face her.

They stared at each other across the short distance, and then her feet moved quickly of their own volition. She flung herself into his open arms, and he squeezed her tight, lifting her from the ground and burying his face in her neck.

"*Mi amor*, I'm sorry," he whispered. "Forgive me, please. I'm losing my mind without you. *Please*."

She nodded, unable to speak because of the glut of emotion

in her throat. Tears sprang to her eyes, and she squeezed them shut.

She didn't know how long they stayed like that, wrapped in each other's arms, but she finally looked up at him with watery eyes. "You're really here for good?"

He nodded. Keeping her in the circle of one arm, his thumb wiped away a tear at the corner of her eye. "I missed you. Damn, I missed you." He kissed her cheeks and lips and chin.

She'd wanted to punish him, but how could she, when he'd uprooted his life for her? When he stood here, in the flesh, begging for forgiveness. When she missed him so much that night after night she prayed for sleep to get a small respite from the ever-present ache in her chest.

Carmen smiled. "I missed you, too. Come up?"

"Absolutely."

21

Carmen was more nervous than Carlos. But of course she was. He was accustomed to having showings over the years, and this was the first time she would attend one with him.

She was so proud of him. He had worked hard to establish a reputation in Toronto. Fortunately, he already had a strong portfolio, a website showcasing his work, and eventually found an agent here in Canada who helped him get established.

Six months had passed quickly, and his hard work paid off, culminating in tonight's exhibition at a prestigious gallery. The walls displayed work he'd completed since his arrival and paintings he'd had shipped from the United States. The show had not officially begun yet, but people had already started trickling in. Off to the side, Carmen watched Carlos engage a potential buyer. The woman nodded as he spoke, and he gestured toward the painting, waving his hand across the width of the canvas as he explained.

His mother and siblings would arrive later, and Carmen's mother had promised to come, as well. Alfred, however, had been noncommittal in his response to the invitation. When he'd learned Carmen had forgiven Carlos and they were not only back together but Carlos had returned to Toronto, he hadn't been pleased. At least he hadn't disowned her or forced her to leave the company.

When the woman walked away, Carlos strolled toward Carmen and she admired his leisurely gait in ripped jeans and a vintage jacket over a white V-neck T-shirt. He'd added a few more silver rings and another bracelet to the collection on his wrist.

He took her hand and smiled. "I think you're more nervous than I am."

She squeezed his fingers. "I am, but I'm also very proud of you."

"I can't wait for my family to get here, my mother especially. This will be the first time she'll see me at a show."

"I know she can't wait. She could barely contain her excitement at dinner the other night," Carmen commented with a laugh. She'd eaten dinner at the Hortados two nights ago. Carlos had still not received an invitation to the Reeves home.

They spent a few minutes chatting with a local artist. Carmen sipped punch as she listened to her and Carlos discuss technique when movement near the door drew her attention. She froze when her father and mother entered the gallery. She and Carlos had expected Graciela to come, but not Alfred. She kept an eye on them as they scanned the walls filled with his paintings.

The gallery owner greeted her parents and handed over one of the flyers. Then Carmen and her father made eye contact, and he and Graciela excused themselves and started in their direction. Alfred's grim expression didn't bode well for the conversation to come. Her mother had probably dragged him there.

"My parents are here," Carmen announced, her stomach knotting up.

Carlos twisted around, and his relaxed pose stiffened somewhat. "Excuse us," he murmured to the other artist, giving her a brief smile.

"Sure. We'll catch up later." She sauntered away.

When her parents stopped in front of them, both couples greeted each other.

"What are you doing here?" Carmen directed the question at her father.

"Last I recall, I was invited," Alfred said.

"I didn't think you'd come."

"Well, I'm here."

"Please don't start anything."

Graciela jumped into the conversation. "He won't. He's genuinely interested in Carlos's work. Isn't that right, *papi*?"

Alfred looked at his wife and then looked at Carmen and Carlos. "That's what your mother wants me to say."

Graciela pressed fingers to her temple and muttered something in Spanish.

"Daddy, please."

"Mr. Reeves—" Carlos stopped talking when Alfred raised a hand.

"Would the three of you let me finish?" His gaze encompassed the small group. "As I was saying, your mother wanted me to say that I was genuinely interested and that's why I came, but frankly, I wasn't interested in Carlos's work. I saw an advertisement for the show and was impressed and realized how talented you are, but that's not why I came. I came because I want to give you something."

Carmen held her breath when he reached into the breast pocket of his jacket. He pulled out a small stack of checks.

"What are those?" she asked.

"Your boyfriend has sent me payments every month. They're all here." Alfred tapped his open palm with the checks.

"You never told me you were doing that," Carmen said, glancing at Carlos. His jaw tightened, but he didn't say a word.

"He has. And every month, I set the check aside, untouched. Six so far, and I imagine another one will arrive next month like the others, and they'll keep arriving until what I gave him over three years ago is paid in full with the interest I told him has accumulated. I came tonight to tell you that you no longer have to send these payments."

Alfred tore the stack in half and then tore those pieces in half. Graciela's mouth fell open, an indication she'd had no idea Alfred planned to do that.

Alfred stuck out the hand containing the torn pieces to Carlos.

Carlos took the checks. "I don't understand."

"My daughter is happy. You owe me nothing." Alfred extended his hand.

Carmen couldn't believe her ears.

Both men shook hands while Graciela and Carmen watched in silence.

"Now I'm going to look at these paintings. Maybe I'll find one I can gift to a friend."

Alfred walked away, leaving Carlos, Carmen, and Graciela staring after him in silence.

Finally, Carmen asked her mother, "Did you have anything to do with this?"

"No. I am as shocked as you are." Graciela gazed up at Carlos. "I am so sorry for what my husband did and for how he made you feel unwelcome. I would love to have you over to the house for dinner one day. If you will accept...?" Her voice trailed off into uncertainty.

"I would like that," Carlos said quietly.

"Good. I'll go join my husband and take a look at your beautiful paintings." Graciela smiled at Carmen. "We will talk later."

"Okay, Mommy." Carmen kissed her mother's cheek.

After her mother walked away, she looked at Carlos.

"I'm still in shock," he said, staring down at the torn papers in his palm.

"Me, too."

Carlos stuck the pieces in his pocket.

"You're keeping them?"

"Yes."

"Why?"

"To remind myself of the mistake I made and what I almost lost." He took her hand and pulled her into a back office.

"What are you doing?" Carmen whispered with a giggle.

Carlos pressed her back against the wall and gave her a slow, sensuous kiss that made her moan. She looped her arms around his neck, swirling her tongue against his, feeling her nipples harden against his firm chest.

Carlos lifted his head. "I wanted a few minutes alone before more people arrive. Then I'll be distracted and won't have time to spend with you. The future is looking better for us, don't you think?"

"Yes," Carmen whispered. "You have your first major show in Toronto, and I'm confident you'll soon be a household name. My father—Alfred Reeves—has *finally* accepted our relationship." She shook her head, still unable to believe what her father had done.

"I'm glad, because I want to marry you, Carmen, and I hated the thought of you having to go against your father's wishes to be with me. I worried that our kids wouldn't be accepted."

"You want to marry me?" she whispered.

"Of course. You knew that, didn't you?"

"I guess I did, but hearing you say it..."

His arms tightened around her waist. "I love you more than anything or anyone else in this world, and I'm going to spend the rest of my life showing you." He gave her a soft kiss, smoothing a hand over her ass. "And one of these days, I'm going to ask you to marry me."

Carmen clutched either side of his jacket and raised up on her toes. "Ask me now."

"No. Not yet."

"*Carlos*."

He chucked softly and kissed her ear. "Be patient, *mi amor*."

Carmen sighed dramatically. "Don't take too long."

"I won't. I love you."

Carmen cupped his jaw and looked deeply into his eyes. "I love you, too."

She was impatient, but there was no need for them to rush. They had their whole lives ahead of them, and she knew without a doubt, they would never be apart again.

ALSO BY DELANEY DIAMOND

Enjoy the other books in the Quicksand series!

A Powerful Attraction (Quicksand #1)

Alex Barraza was only supposed to have dinner with his employee, Sherry Westbrook, but their attraction cannot be denied. They decide to keep their affair a secret, but what happens when Sherry learns the truth about him?

Without You (Quicksand #2)

After years of cheating, Charisse finally walked away from Terrence "T-Murder" Burrell, but he wants her back. When trust is broken, can it ever be repaired?

Never Again (Quicksand #3)

Carlos Hortado receives a second chance to be with the woman he left three years ago. But he has a secret. When Carmen finds out, will she be the one to walk away this time?

Free short stories available at www.delaneydiamond.com.

ABOUT THE AUTHOR

Delaney Diamond is the USA Today Bestselling Author of sweet, sensual, passionate romance novels. Originally from the U.S. Virgin Islands, she now lives in Atlanta, Georgia. She reads romance novels, mysteries, thrillers, and a fair amount of nonfiction. When she's not busy reading or writing, she's in the kitchen trying out new recipes, dining at one of her favorite restaurants, or traveling to an interesting locale.

Enjoy free reads and the first chapter of all her novels on her website. Join her mailing list to get sneak peeks, notices of sale prices, and find out about new releases.

Join her mailing list
www.delaneydiamond.com

facebook.com/DelaneyDiamond
twitter.com/DelaneyDiamond
instagram.com/authordelaneydiamond
BB bookbub.com/authors/delaney-diamond
pinterest.com/delaneydiamond

www.ingramcontent.com/pod-product-compliance
Lightning Source LLC
Chambersburg PA
CBHW072229190626
46809CB00017B/1597

* 9 7 8 1 9 4 6 3 0 2 1 3 7 *